RISE
OF
LEGENDS

CHOSEN LEGENDS

BOOK 1

AJ DASHER & KRIS RUHLER

GPV

PUBLISHING

ALSO BY

Kris Ruhler

YA Science Fantasy – Aeterna Chronicles

Prequel 1: Shackles of Guilt

Prequel 2: Severed Ties

Book 1: Strands of Time

Book 2: Coils of Revenge

Book 3: Shattered Souls

Book 4: Fractured Bonds

Book 5: Scorched Threads

Book 6: Raging Tides

YA Superhero Urban Fantasy – Chosen Legends

Prequel: Slivers of Memory

Book 1: Rise of Legends

RISE OF LEGENDS

Book 2: Threads of Illusion (Coming Soon!)

YA Epic Fantasy – Shadow and Ruin

Book 1: Quest of Shadow and Ruin

Book 2: Coming Soon

Publisher: GPV Publishing

First Edition: September 2023

ASIN: B0CGVRVKZT

ISBN: 979-8860684898

AUTHOR'S NOTE

My "writing journey," as it's often referred to, was rather chaotic.

And I mean *quite* chaotic. My writing was all over the place. From silly jokes to flowery language, nothing made sense to me. Perhaps it still doesn't. After all, I began writing when I was five years old, and in one decade, I've made a ton of improvement.

Nevertheless, all that nonsense still got me somewhere. It had me writing, pencil on paper (I know for certain that Kris HATES pencils because it doesn't show up well on paper, but hear me out, alright—my handwriting was bad, and I always made spelling mistakes, so OBVIOUSLY, I needed an eraser because scribbling makes things look absolutely horrible.)

After I'd written all my ideas down on paper, I tried to put them into an actual story.

It was April 2019 when I first started writing Chosen Legends. My first couple of drafts didn't even have a proper plan. But I wrote three books, all around 20K words, and then they were expanded into six separate books. Then, I reached out to Kris for help; I told her I didn't know what to do. My ideas were all over the place, but I *needed* to get them out of my head. I *needed* to have them make sense to others. I was a silly ten-year-old who didn't know how to write, so what could one really expect from me?

But Kris read my writing. She said once she was done writing her debut series, *Aeterna Chronicles*, she would help me write my books. At the time, I'd read ARCs of her books and was reading her fifth book, *Scorched Threads*. I loved her world-building and characters, and I still do! So, some of me hoped that she would see even just an ounce of worth in my writing. And she did. Nothing could've made me happier than that. If I ever thought of my ideas as stones, they soon became gems I learned to cherish.

The same year, in July, after I turned eleven, I found the motivation to write.

The original copy of Chosen Legends was called "Chosen Zero," which was a stand-alone rather than a series. In my "past life," as I like to call it, I was foolish enough to never make copies when I re-wrote something, so everything was in one file.

It still baffles me how much my writing has changed since 2019. It doesn't feel that long ago (bear with me; I know it's been four and a half years.)

There were many things wrong with the original copy that Kris went through. The main characters' names were weird, the plot was all over the place, and everything moved too quickly. That explained why the second book was only twenty thousand words. If only I expanded it, wrote good descriptions, and developed the characters, it probably would've been at least eighty thousand words.

Of course, I didn't do that. Did I mention I was foolish?

Yet, somehow, it worked out. And I couldn't have done that without Kris.

Then we published Slivers of Memory, and it was on a school day. I came to school for celebrations and congratulations from my friends and teachers, and that was probably one of the best moments in my life—becoming an author was a dream I had, and my dream had come true. And if you're a fellow writer, trust me; keep writing, editing, and reaching for that goal. After a while, seeing your ideas out there for everyone to read about (physical or digital book) makes it worthwhile.

I'd also like to thank my friends (who, I will admit, are goofy and have the craziest ideas sometimes) for giving me the motivation to write. Although most of my thoughts had been finalized before even writing, and despite the constant madness of being around them, I feel at ease being around friends and family.

Amidst this beautiful chaos is where I find joy.

I hope that you, my dear reader, will find joy as well.

Enjoy the read!

Join me on my Instagram account @ajdasherauthor.

About Rise of
Legends

**An ancient threat is rising. The fate of the Legends is
sealed.**

For Michael Jacobs, high school is hard enough. He just
wants to be invisible.

But everything changes when bullies chase him to an
abandoned building, and a near-death experience trig-
gers a strange, new power.

Except his luck isn't going to last. A new organization
in the city threatens the peace, and he soon becomes
their target.

That's not all.

An ancient, vengeful monster, buried in the distant
stars of a faraway galaxy is awakening, its quest for power
ruthless. Worse still, it has big plans to get to Earth... with
Michael on its radar.

Entangled in this web of danger and on the run,
Michael finds two allies and has no choice but to follow

them into the unknown. With their help and a dash of luck, he might just have a fighting chance to survive.

Bursting with action, Rise of Legends *is the first book in the* Chosen Legends *series.*

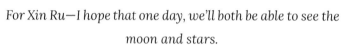

For Xin Ru—I hope that one day, we'll both be able to see the moon and stars.
Thank you for being there for me.

PROLOGUE

Westview Day 1, afternoon.

F alling...

What would you do if you were pulled down four hundred feet by the full force of gravity?

All that goes up must come down. My physics teacher, Mr. Hoffmann, had rambled on about Newton's laws earlier today.

Forget the sci-fi movies, kids; nothing ever floats except balloons, bubbles, and matter less dense than air... It's a simple natural law. Superman is just a farce, deal with it. The Earth's core is a pretty nasty magnet.

Mr. Hoffmann, with his white hair and eccentric attitude, had got that right. That was where it all started: gravity. No, my fate had been sealed much earlier, before school started.

The ground shot up toward me like an angry giant's mouth growling for my flesh. A horrifying fall from the fifteen-story building at the west end of Golden Birch—was how I was going to die.

The building had been abandoned for two reasons: first, a giant sinkhole had collapsed the front wall. Second, it used to be a hospital, but the rumor was that it was just a cover. Something terrible had happened there. Just my luck that I chose this building to hide in.

I was hurtling toward said sinkhole at breakneck speed, like a pile of trash emptying into a trashy trash can. Of course, it had been an accident, I told myself, when I tried to escape from Jack, Kyle, and Zachary. The floor was slippery and slanted from the collapse. None of the boys would have pushed me off that really high building—at least, not intentionally. They only wanted to scare me and had me cornered at the very edge when it happened. Right? That was what I told myself over and over again, like a broken recording.

I freefell like a crashing aircraft that had lost its vital controls. With the wind rushing in my ears, the sting in my eyes, and the panicking, I could already envisage the sharp pain that would follow almost immediately: the crunching of bones, the ugly splattering of blood over the sidewalk, and the gruesome dismembering of my body which would be scattered like torn bits of paper. Maybe I'd end up as a bloody pancake. And there was absolutely nothing I could do about it now—absolutely nothing.

The thought of my foster parents, the Jacobs, flashed into my mind. They had been so kind to take me in. I tried to cling to the other happy memories of my fourteen years. Well, there weren't that many—almost impossible to find since half of my life had been scattered throughout orphanages and living on the streets and off scraps.

With its huge dark mouth, the ground shot up like a struck baseball toward my face.

Here comes the pain.

Then, the strangest thing happened. The fall slowed, and so did time itself. Maybe that explained why so many thoughts crossed my mind in such a short time.

Which was a good thing, as an abrupt stop would be like slamming into a brick wall. Like a car going at a hundred miles an hour and then coming to a halt. My organs, which already felt like mushy dough, were like the driver not wearing a seatbelt slowly crashing through the windshield.

An object in motion stays in motion with the same speed and in the same direction were Mr. Hoffmann's words. The Law of Inertia. Great.

The ground was still approaching too fast. My arms flailed in an attempt to shield my face; my stomach climbed into my throat. No way would I survive this fall.

Suddenly, time, which had been slowing down, came to a stop. The ticking hands on my watch stopped, and my breath caught in my throat. The wind rushing at me turned into a breeze, and the hairs on my arms froze.

Maybe this was what death felt like. Not that many people came back from the dead to tell about it. And those who did talked about tunneling light vision in the last few seconds of their lives.

No one had ever said anything about a pair of red, reptilian eyes staring back at them.

For a moment, I was suspended mid-air like a floating balloon, just levitating there as if some sort of invisible string was pulling me up like a puppet. All I could do was stare at the twin points of red lights. Pretty sure I wasn't bungee jumping from that abandoned building.

This is it, was my final thought. *I must be dead.*

CHAPTER 1

Day 1, morning

In the morning, before I ended up not-bungee-jumping from a building, I woke up with a tingling feeling in my hands and toes and a massive headache. Stay home and mope around, or go to school? Nah, I had a perfect attendance record, and reports were out this week. No way was I slacking off.

Anyway, the smell of waffles wafting into my bedroom made my stomach growl. So I staggered out of bed, had a quick wash, and put on dark blue jeans and a beige shirt. Donning such an outfit would surely blend me in with Golden Birch High School's walls. Which was perfectly fine.

I bounded down the stairs and nearly stumbled over a stack of suitcases. Oh, right... It was *that* day. My heart sank. It was like a hand had reached into my chest and squeezed the breath out of me. But I shook my head. I had no right to be sad. Or did I?

Still, I tried smiling at Janet and Mark Jacobs, my foster parents, a task that required massive effort. Stuffing my mouth with waffles and washing it down with orange juice gave me the perfect excuse not to talk. But I couldn't avoid their concerned gazes.

For the first time in the seven years since they'd adopted me, they were going on holiday. By themselves.

"Morning, Michael! You look a bit pale," Janet said, pouring more batter into the waffle maker.

I nodded, picked up a waffle, and chewed noisily.

"You'll send us your grades, won't you?" Mark asked absently, squinting at the screen in his hand, currently displaying a bot prototype. He loved building and fixing stuff.

I nodded again and regretted it when Janet sighed out of frustration. Sometimes, finding the right words was the most difficult thing.

You have no right to ruin everything with your whining, I told myself. Nor should I be envious that they were heading away for two whole long weeks. Without me.

Janet was still watching me, clearly expecting a response. When I remained silent, she gave another suffering sigh. "Michael."

I glanced up at her over my stack of waffles. "Janet."

Her glare made the food in my mouth turn dry. "Don't sass me."

I took a gulp of orange juice. *You should be grateful.*

These guys took you in—a scrawny seven-year-old. They gave you a roof and food and everything you could ask for. A double-bladed pocketknife, an advanced digital notebook, even that weird metal binder that was perfect for hitting people over the head with. Plus, we went on holiday for two weeks every year.

This year is just...different.

"I said I'm fine." Yikes. My voice came out more forcefully than I meant it to.

Janet scoffed and waved at her husband in disbelief. "Mark. Come on."

Mark hardly glanced up from his phone. "Mhm. Sounds good, honey."

"Mark!" She hissed, and he was startled at her tone.

He gave me a helpless look. "Uh. Michael, you sure you're alright?"

I gritted my teeth. "Okay, this is starting to feel like an interrogation." As if to make a point, I shoved another waffle in my mouth. Honestly, if I weren't so hungry, I'd have left the conversation by now.

Janet and Mark were good parents. Apparently, they just needed some "us" time together—just the two of them. Whatever that meant.

So, since this was the last week before break and plane ticket prices soared in five days, Janet had decided it was the perfect time for a break. In fact, she went ahead and booked their flight. Mark, placid as ever, agreed. The poor guy did try to protest that the resort was totally disconnected from the internet. No news, no streaming. But Janet remained firm. Now, the two of them were heading to this quiet resort this very evening.

And since I had a good view of the office from the kitchen, I was sure Janet hadn't packed his bulky books either. Poor Mark was going to have to make conversation for so many days.

Janet poured syrup over the waffle on her plate. "You're fourteen and responsible enough. And you know how to call the street patrol bots. Don't worry—Katie, the babysitter I've hired, will take care of anything you need. You're going to be just fine."

Sure. Not like I was having any parties while they were MIA (although I'd bet my whole knife collection that they'd actually like that I throw a party and invite my tons and tons of non-existent friends). But I figured with the wad of cash they were leaving me and some budgeting, I could treat myself to doing whatever I wanted to. For a whole fourteen days. Plus, I didn't need a babysitter. I'd have to find a way to ditch them.

Yeah. I can be happy I get the house all to myself.

Yet the misery in my gut didn't let up. I was pretty good at being invisible. If I were to follow them to the resort, they'd never know I was around. Then, a thought occurred to me, and my hand froze midway to my mouth. Me being invisible would defeat the purpose, right? I'd still be alone. I couldn't help the envy, though, watching the suitcases and bags sprawled about in the living room.

A sudden stabbing pain in my head made me gasp, and the waffle fell from my hand onto the plate. Mark looked up from his screen, frowning. For a moment, I thought of telling him about this strange ache. But the only thing that came out of my mouth was a muffled 'Sorry.'

"We'll be right here when you get back from school," Janet said. "Our flight is at nine." She looked over at Mark. "Honey, do you really have to go to work today?"

"It was a last-minute decision," Mark replied. "I have some projects to tie up."

I'd known Mark for seven years, but even a stranger would've noticed his tight voice. He was the kind to be really annoyed about last-minute decisions. But Janet smiled, took a sip of her coffee, and returned to the waffle maker.

I'd always found their dynamic funny. While Janet was all jittery nerves, Mark was the impassive, non-verbal type. He ambled around the kitchen while sipping his coffee, all composed, while Janet skittered about. They complemented one another, like peanut butter and jelly.

But now Janet wanted more 'chatting,' and knowing

Mark, it would be a hard task to achieve. They'd probably work it out eventually. They always did.

My stomach churned as I swallowed the syrupy waffles. The tingling returned, and my fingers tightened on the fork to stop them from shaking. It was more like pins and needles, the kind you got when your legs fell asleep, and you started moving. The pins-and-needles feeling faded away, leaving a dull ache behind. It wasn't painful, but damn, it was annoying—like an itch I couldn't get rid of

Was I sick? Was there something wrong with my nervous system? The strange thing was that I'd never been sick—hence my perfect attendance record. For the seven years I'd been at the Jacobs, not even a sniffle. Even before that, while living in the orphanages or on the streets, nothing.

Maybe I should take the day off. What was the point of a perfect attendance record, anyway? I wasn't going to get an award for it. With my average grades and average skills, I wasn't really good at anything. Maybe I should let Janet know.

"Michael? Got your coat?" she asked, flipping an egg in the frying pan. I hadn't even noticed the eggs; I'd been so absorbed in my thoughts.

Janet's blond curls caught a ray of summer sunshine as she spun around to look at me with her pale blue eyes.

I looked nothing like her. Not with my dark eyes, shaggy brown hair, and pale skin.

"It looks bright out there," I mumbled. "Don't need a coat." I sounded like a sulking kid.

But there was something that flickered in her eyes that struck me. Behind the concern was guilt and doubt.

Nope, I couldn't tell her about my stupid tingling. I couldn't stay at home either. It would give her the perfect excuse to cancel their getaway.

"It's always good to be prepared, right?" she said.

Now, she was avoiding looking at me altogether. To be honest, while I'd hidden my resentment, Janet had looked guilty for days. She scooped the eggs onto a plate and sat down at the table. Mark didn't even look up.

"You got everything? Lunch money? I left cash in the cupboard. I've got frozen meals—enough for ten dinners. Maybe more. And about your school report, I wish—"

She always spoke too fast when she was feeling emotional. Suddenly, I wanted the two of them to fix whatever was going on between them. I ignored the shiver trailing down my spine and the persistent pins and needles. My discomfort would have to wait. She really cared for me, and I wanted her to be happy.

So I smiled and forced myself to relax. "I'll be all right, Janet. I'll send you guys a text every day. And I'll scan my report and send it too, okay? Don't worry at all and enjoy your trip. You both deserve it."

My wide, beaming smile had the desired effect. Her hunched shoulders drooped a tad bit, and the little 'V' between her eyebrows disappeared.

"Oh, the bus is here!" she shouted. "Be back before six. The taxi's picking us up at quarter past!"

"And be safe out there," Mark added, looking up. "School's a minefield these days."

Considering how I'd been dodging bullies in the past week, he was spot on. In his own way, he cared for me, too.

I grabbed three more waffles, my coat, and my backpack and dashed to the door, my mouth too full to reply. A bully on the streets once took all my food scraps—leftovers from a fast food that I'd been saving up. So my motto was: eat whenever you can; you never know who'll steal it from you and when's the next meal.

A wave from afar. That was all I gave them. I wished I'd hugged them and let them know how much I loved them. How much I loved Janet reading about the archaic Supervengers to me every night and teaching me about the big, wide world and what there was to know. As I'd started school late, she'd made sure that I was all caught up, and I knew all the stuff that seven-year-olds did and much more. Or Mark teaching me how to use a drill and screwdriver while we put up a bookshelf. Helping me fix everything and anything we could get our hands on.

I wished I'd given the Jacobs a proper goodbye.

If only I'd known that I'd never see them again.

CHAPTER 2

As I stepped onto the school bus, all I could think of was getting rid of the strange sensation coursing through my veins. Surely, it'd be over soon. Better yet, it'd be over by the time school started. And just like that, as the thought crossed my mind, the pins and needles suddenly stopped. Victory at last.

Unfortunately, by the time the bus swerved into Golden Birch High School's parking lot, the strange, dull ache had started again. Not only that, but—you know what goosebumps feel like? Cold shivers down your arms? It was like that, only it wasn't cold. Warmth spread down from my shoulders. My arms felt as if they were close to an oven. Again—not painful but still annoying. Was I having a fever?

Maybe I was coming down with something. Maybe some cold water would help. Maybe I was *dying*. Oh, well. I had ten minutes before the bell, so I headed for the water fountain at the end of the hall.

I had to admit that I would miss school during the break. I had no plans or clue what to do for a whole week alone at home. I had no friends. Although, I guess I liked it better that way. Chatting about trivial things grated on my nerves.

What I'd really miss was learning new stuff, especially science—even though I sucked at all my subjects. I even failed math despite countless hours of studying.

At least the stars and constellations could provide me with some comfort this break. Janet got me this fantastic telescope with incredible magnitude. What better time to test it out? There was this long-dead scientist who, decades ago, said how we are cosmically connected to the stars. I wanted to believe that.

As I walked down the corridor, I caught my reflection in the window overlooking the courtyard. My clothes screamed stereotypical slacker: dark blue jeans, an off-white, almost beige, long-sleeved shirt, and black and red Converse sneakers. Average height, average build, and no sense of fashion. My arm tingled again with that annoying sensation, and I did my best to subtly shake it off.

I strived to be nobody. Because what I learned from high school was this: don't look like someone who can easily be tackled to the ground. Keep your head down.

Lost in my thoughts, I was still ambling toward the

fountain when something in the courtyard outside the window drew my attention. My feet froze, and it was like all my senses were on alert.

Jack and his gang. I'd been avoiding them all week since the gym incident. The No-Brains trio may not have the sharpest brains—or any brains at all, really. But when they got humiliated—which was, unfortunately, my doing—somehow, they never forgot about it.

I shifted and saw that the trio surrounded a small figure. Another poor soul was about to lose their lunch money if they had any on them.

I was about to turn away when a blue streak of light flashed across the tarmac outside. Curious, I drew close to the door. I was about to open it, my hand on the handle, when a little bolt of electricity crackled over the handle and weaved around my hand like a rope before I could move away. I jumped, and my addled brain thought too late that this bolt should have fried my hand. Yet, instead of jerking my hand away, it actually froze on the handle. Like it had a mind of its own.

The weird thing was that my entire arm felt energized, and the tingling sensation was gone.

That should have been my cue to stay away. Instead, I twisted the handle and opened the door. My legs, just like my hand, moved as if they had a will of their own, carrying me outside. In full view of Jack and his gang.

I wasn't stupid. This was trouble I'd usually avoid. So, what on Earth was I doing?

The air hung heavy as if a thunderstorm was approaching. Yet the blue, cloudless sky belied the sensation. The goosebumps on my arms had nothing to do with fear. It felt like I had wings and had ingested one of these energy drinks. I was ready to face anyone and everyone. Even Jack.

A little voice inside me screamed, *Mind your own business! Survive this place for five days, and then you'll have a break. Jack will have forgotten all about it by then. No more bullies. No more Jack, Kyle, or Zachary.*

My first encounter with Jack went as follows:

Jack (shouting in the hall): Heard you ate from dumpsters.

Me (seconds later): How—? No! I never did that!

Those five words he uttered ruined my school life. It was as if these high schoolers craved gossip, and the new rumor was poor little orphan me, acting like a raccoon on the streets.

I never ate from dumpsters. Sure, I had my own way of finding food—stealing and finding leftovers. And yeah, I used to break into people's homes if times got desperate. I was the slippery kid from the streets that the cops never caught. The one who knew all the exits and was gone the second they looked away. The kid with secret hideouts in the alleyways. But no matter how much I had, I always shared my loot with other kids on the street who always got picked on by bullies like Jack. Bullies like Kyle who were much stronger and faster.

Back on the streets, there had been a group of us who cared for each other. Ben, Amy, and I.

That had been my life before I ended up in an orphanage. I thought that I'd created a new life with the Jacobs and left my old one behind. But bullies seemed to follow me wherever I went. And now, I'm alone.

Turn away, man, you don't want trouble. You're not a hero. As I drew closer to the gang, I stopped in my tracks as memories of the gym incident from a few days ago came forth.

Friday. Gym class. I was running around the perimeter during dodgeball, keeping away from the other players, when the weirdest thing happened. You know when the ball comes at you, and you wish it didn't as all the other players converge on you with murder in their eyes?

Yep, the ball flew straight toward my face. Some doofus threw it at me before he got tackled to the ground. I swore my heart skipped a beat, and I stopped breathing. Heart pounding, I watched in horror as the ball sailed toward me.

I squeezed my eyes tightly shut and braced for impact—well, in dodgeball, you're supposed to dodge, but that was the last thing on my mind. If I caught it, I'd be tackled. If I didn't, I might have a chance to survive.

The ball never reached me.

A mix of emotions ensued. Relief that the ball was far away from me. Confusion that I was no longer the target. Surprise to see Jack, who was on the other side, knocked off his feet by the ball rebounding off him. From the few players shaking their heads at my stupidity, I knew something terrible had happened. I could swear that neither my hands nor any part of my body made contact with that ball. But who would believe me?

Jack got back to his feet, fists clenched and glaring at me. Then he stomped in my direction.

That was when the coach shouted orders for a break and—*ooof!* Never had I felt such relief. Jack probably wouldn't have done anything in front of the coach, but I wasn't taking any chances.

Back to the present, where my feet picked up the pace of their own accord.

"Hey, Jack." The words came out of me. Darn, I even sounded like I was meeting him at a school reunion or something. Casual and too familiar.

As the burly, athletic boy turned to me in the court-yard, his fierce look indicated he hadn't forgotten about the gym incident. I thought of telling him that I'd never hit him—that the ball might have just sort of bounced off me—but heck, even I couldn't explain it.

Out of the corner of my eye, little shoots of electricity zipped across the ground. Blue shoots, the kind you see sparking from a dangling cable after a storm. How weird. Jack and the others seemed unaffected by the sight, even as I was mesmerized. The hairs on my forearm began to rise as the air became charged. The surge was exhilarating as if I could *absorb* the electricity.

Then, the other two bullies turned to flank me. *Um, no. No way, nope. Michael, what are you doing?! What happened to your survival skills?*

But something weighed on my chest now—a compelling and completely mad feeling. I knew for certain that I shouldn't—couldn't—leave. Call it instinct or sixth sense. But that sensation had saved my life many times before.

My gaze fell on the small figure behind Jack, watching me with a curious gaze. Wavy, shoulder-length brown hair, hazel eyes, and white alabaster skin.

Allegra. We had English class together. Seeing her sent my thoughts skittering. Maybe her presence in the courtyard explained why I felt so compelled. Second, my heart started racing, and despite the cold drizzle, warmth spread down my arms. Everything around me faded away, and it was only her. Such a fascinating—

Hold on. She and her dreadful twin sister, Alex, always hung out together. But Alex, with her spiky brown hair and annoying attitude, was nowhere to be seen.

Allegra's eyes were defiant, her chin raised. She looked as if a storm would burst out of her.

"Leave her alone, Jack," I blurted out before logic could catch up. My mouth and brain needed to have a serious conversation between themselves after this. "Stop picking on people."

Allegra smiled, white teeth flashing. My breath caught in my throat like I'd been struck by lightning. Maybe I had been, because these little blue sparks were on my bare arms. But Allegra just beamed as if I had just offered her the world.

The air lightened for a fraction of a second, and I took a deep breath. No turning back now. What the heck was I thinking? *Please let me get away with this just once.*

Jack snickered, unfazed by my intrusion. He cracked his knuckles as his goons closed in, all three looming over me like mountains. Actually, I was only an inch shorter than them. The looming effect was kind of lost on me.

"Were you about to go dumpster diving, Mikey? Looking for scraps in the garbage, where you belong?"

I hated it when Kyle called me Mikey.

"No, but with that stench on you, I could ask you the same thing." Did my mouth just tell Kyle, the looming giant, that he smelled nasty? It was true, but—

Ah, screw it. What am I supposed to do now?

I glanced around. No one was coming to help. Just a few kids who pointedly ignored us, too afraid of Jack's reign of terror.

The bully's fist scrunched up the front of my shirt and yanked me closer. I clawed at the arm holding me up but to no avail. It was like fighting a tree trunk. Jack's free arm reared back, a sickening smile on his face.

The silver lining was that Allegra was intact and safe. As long as their attention was on me, she had a chance to get out of there unharmed. The air became ionized again, heavier than before. The blue flashes of light crackled on the ground in a violent dance.

"You see that blue light on the ground?" I asked Jack.

For a moment, he looked confused at my lack of fear, then his mouth twisted. "What, you trying to distract me?"

"Leave them alone, Jack!" a voice boomed across the field.

To my surprise, Jack let go of my shirt. It was so sudden that I staggered backward and fell to the ground. My back ached with the promise of fresh bruises. But a few seconds later, I was on my feet and saw Alex and a boy I didn't recognize trailing behind her.

The following chain of events left me bewildered.

All three bullies suddenly held their heads in their

hands, moaning with pain as if gripped with brutal migraines. A throbbing pain built up in my head, too, but it was bearable.

I managed to keep my head up and stay put as Jack and his gang left the courtyard, throwing fearful glances at Alex. Like I said, it was a bewildering sight. Alex was easily half the size of Kyle.

Alex glared at her sister, ignoring me. "I told you to stay by my side!" she growled.

Allegra crossed her arms and glared back. The two girls were fraternal twins, but the physical resemblance was still uncanny. Both had hazel eyes and chestnut hair. But while Alex looked at everyone with murder in her eyes, it was Allegra who made my heart race.

The latter turned to me and smiled. For a moment, I held my breath, stunned. Maybe it was the heavy air or just the sight of her glowing face. But she was the most beautiful thing I'd ever seen.

Then Alex whipped toward me, eyes as fierce as a lioness. I didn't move a muscle at all.

"You!" she said between gritted teeth, pointing an accusatory finger at me. "Stay away from her."

But then something drew my attention. "Is that a dog?" It was one of the cutest things I'd seen in a while, with its long, thin face and big eyes.

"What dog?" Alex growled again.

"Oh," Allegra started.

When I looked again behind Alex, there was no dog, and the boy who was behind her just a few moments ago had also vanished. Was I hallucinating?

Both girls were gone before I could come up with an explanation. The air became lighter, and the blue sparks were gone. Even the sky brightened up with sun rays around the courtyard. Yeah, no. Bewilderment couldn't even begin to describe this turn of events.

The bell rang, shaking me out of stupor, and I headed back toward the entrance door.

I caught sight of two men in orange robes loitering near the entrance doors. They must be stage actors. It was the last day of school, after all.

I thought what happened in gym class was terrible. Now, it just got worse. How was I going to avoid Jack and his gang for five days? I should've stayed home.

The tipping point was during science class.

I enjoyed Mr. Hoffmann's classes—so much better than having holo teachers. His wild white hair was dull under the ugly fluorescent lighting as he announced a surprise pop quiz. He liked to do them on the fly and just call out questions. It was a challenge to our brilliant minds, he'd say. But to our mediocre minds, his pop quizzes were anything but. Long silences usually reigned during these quizzes as everyone dug into their brains for answers. I was one of the few who'd utter anything—for extra marks, even though I'd often get the answers partially wrong.

"You, sitting at the back!" Mr. Hoffmann suddenly shouted. "Yes, the one drooling with your head tipped back. Let me hear you define gravity."

I turned to see Jack blink several times, his eyes dazed. For a moment, I felt pity for the poor guy. Science was a compulsory class, and everybody knew Jack was failing it.

Jack's gaze swept from side to side. It fell on Kyle, but Mr. Hoffmann was drawing closer and blocked his view. The teacher was almost next to his desk and looming over the poor guy when, to Jack's misfortune, he sputtered out, "A place where dead people are buried?"

A thick silence followed. Mr. Hoffmann crossed his arms and waited. Then he sighed like Jack was a lost cause—which, in hindsight, was humiliating—turned around and headed back to the front of the class. You could hear a pin drop in the silence, save for a snicker from a student.

It was to *my* misfortune that the snicker had come from me. To add to the problem, Mr. Hoffmann's attention latched onto me, and I was forced to stutter out the correct answer: *gravity is the universal force of attraction between all matter*. Of course, I got awarded bonus marks, but it was pitiful compared to what now awaited me.

I was so dead.

After school, at the first ring of the bell, I was out and darting toward the bus. Where, of course, the three bullies awaited.

CHAPTER 3

Day 1, afternoon

C all me a coward, but I knew when I was out-matched. So, I ditched the school bus and took the long way home. I calculated it would take me less than an hour to get back, giving me plenty of time to see the Jacobs off.

As I turned around the last corner of my street with all its nice cookie-cutter houses, I caught sight of Kyle's blond hair and ducked. Darn luck. All three bullies were loitering close to my house. Go around and get in through the backdoor? No way would I be able to get inside quickly before they tackled me to the ground.

How did they find my address? It must be Jack's doing. He was the son of the principal. It would've been easy for him to sneak into the school office and get the info. It bothered me that he would go to such lengths. It also meant I was up for a serious beating.

After some thought, I decided to move away and wait it out. The No-Brains trio would grow tired and move on.

Or so I hoped.

In the middle of Golden Birch, close to the city hall, was Broadway Park, the largest open space in the city and close enough to my house. So, I quickly moved away. Part of me fumed for being targeted like that. I didn't deserve it. Another part of me was dejected that I couldn't say goodbye to Janet and Mark.

I checked my watch. Two more hours to waste till the taxi arrived. Maybe if I headed back before six, I could still be on time for the goodbyes. My phone pinged, but I ignored it. Janet must be wondering why I missed the bus. If I didn't turn up, they'd think I was still sulking. Which I wasn't. I just wanted to avoid certain death.

The park came into view. It was always so quiet, which gave me a sense of peace. Like a sanctuary. I breathed in the fresh air right as a car zipped past.

With the advent of a new electro catalyst for turning carbon dioxide into liquid fuel, the city was now teeming with pollution-free cars—goodbye diesel and fossil fuels. People were even talking about flying cars now—for the common people, of course, since the super-rich already had aero taxis. Planes and things floating in the sky, defying physics and gravity—including Superman—had always awed me.

I sat down on a swing, alert and on the lookout for three burly figures. Out of the corner of my eye, I saw kids playing with their robots, mothers pushing their strollers, and a couple of teens giggling in a hologram conference. Nothing unusual. Yet, I couldn't shake the feeling of being watched. That sixth sense of mine was warning me of my impending doom.

My stomach growled. I pushed the thought of food from my mind and instead thought about Allegra and that incredible surge of energy I'd felt this morning. The tingling in my hands and toes was gone. Something had pulled me toward her like gravity holding the solar system in balance. Hard to understand why I'd stand up for someone I'd never talked to. Ever. Even if I *did* have a teensy-weensy crush on them.

What was that electrifying feeling? Why the sudden, fierce need to stand between her and the bullies?

Now I understood why Janet would fuss over me, her worries when I came back with a bruised knee or a bump on the head. Her constant attention and coddling were annoying, but I let her be. It made her happy to take care of me. At that thought, a pang of guilt stabbed me. She was waiting for me.

I took out my phone and texted a quick 'Went out with friends. Be back soon.'

Sitting alone on the swing, I realized I had no one to care for. No siblings. No friends. It felt *good* to stand up to Jack and protect Allegra. Something unfurled inside me, although I didn't know what.

I buried the feeling before I got carried away. Around me, the mothers pushed their strollers out of the park, and the children left the climbing frames. Maybe it was time for me to head back home, too.

My phone pinged, and I scrolled through my messages. Janet urging me to get back home soon. Mark giving me the thumbs up for having friends. Ugh.

I searched for Allegra, an inexplicable longing to see her again. A class photo popped up. I stared at the grainy picture and the girl with hazel eyes. There was no other info on socials other than the Golden Birch High School she and her sister were registered at only a few months ago. It was as if the two sisters didn't exist or didn't attend school before. How strange.

"There he is!" a loud, husky voice thundered on my right.

I looked up to see Zachary pointing at me. Right behind him were Kyle and Jack, grinning wildly like a clown.

I hurriedly put my phone in the pocket of my baggy jeans and started to run, but Jack was already standing a few paces before me. A red bandanna was tied around his auburn hair, and his glare was fiercer than ever.

"You hiding from me, little Mikey? We got something unresolved from this morning."

When Jack used words he didn't know the meaning

of—like "unresolved"—he was surely up to no good. Was it my fault that he couldn't remember what gravity was or that he couldn't catch a ball? I wondered how deep in trouble one could get, because I was far beyond that.

"You were ganging up on that small girl," I hissed through clenched teeth. "Why don't you pick on someone your own size?" Again, why did my mouth keep uttering words? Why couldn't I keep it shut?

"Ganging up? That's my new girlfriend you're talking about."

"Say what?" Allegra was Jack's girlfriend? Oh god, I was thinking about her lunch money being stolen.

"Yeah, I was asking her out when you interrupted. What's your problem?"

"I don't think she said yes—" Kyle started. He stopped when Jack glowered in his direction.

"You just have to ruin everything, don't you?" Jack asked, his left fist thudding into his other palm and his eyes boring daggers into me.

Without warning, he threw a punch at me. But I'd seen this coming since Friday. I ducked and stepped away, my fingers clutching the shoulder straps of my backpack.

I should've kept away from them, never gotten involved. Another blow came, but I dodged it, weaved again, and took another step back. I was cornered, flanked by a pole and a tree behind me.

Another punch flew at me. This time, I wasn't fast enough. Unexpectedly, Kyle's other hand grabbed my hair and shoved my face against the nearby pole.

Pain exploded in my right cheekbone and forehead. Blood trickled from my nose as I turned around. All I could do was grip the pole to stop from staggering and falling to the ground.

Then Zachary, the burliest of the three, came at me. I dodged his punch, and his fist slammed into the metal pole. Wincing and with tears in his eyes, he shook his hand from the split skin on his knuckles.

Jack stepped back, crouched down, and picked up my phone that had fallen from my pocket. His snicker turned into a scowl as he saw Allegra's photo on the screen. With clenched fists, he looked up and glared.

"What? You stalking my girlfriend now? Man, you asked for it!"

"She's not your girl—" I clamped my teeth down on my tongue hard, and the taste of iron filled my mouth. I deserved it. Seriously, I needed to shut up.

Both Kyle and Zachary stepped away from Jack like someone would do in the presence of a bomb about to explode. They might be his so-called friends, but they knew well when he was close to bursting. I was right under his nose and about to take the brunt of his temper.

And with a pole on one side, a bench on the other, and a tree blocking the exit behind me, I was helpless.

"Apologize, you idiot!" Kyle shouted from a distance away. Good advice. His shifty eyes told me it was more of a warning. "Give us your money," he added quickly, "and we'll be out of your hair. You know how this works."

I had to give Kyle credit for trying to give me an out, but I had no money. I made a mental note to carry all my cash with me later. Assuming there was a later.

Jack grabbed the front of my shirt and pulled me closer. "I can do this all day," he said, his eyes on the left side of my face that must be bruising. I could practically feel the heat of his increasing rage.

"Patrol b-bots are coming," I managed to get out. My throat felt tight. That earned me another punch to my eye. Ouch. That stung.

"You think the patrol drones will protect you?" Jack shot back. He glanced around the park—deserted other than a lone mother and her child who had their backs to us and were woefully too far away to hear us. My hope that some kind citizen would see the scene and alert the patrol died.

"You got what's coming next," Jack hissed in my ear. "Throwing a ball at me, mocking me. I'm going to beat you to a pulp! And you know what," he leaned in, the foul scent of his breath assaulting my nose, "you're going to *thank* me after. You're going to be *grateful* for your life."

My gaze met with Kyle's. His eyes were filled with pity, while Zachary just averted his, pretending to be looking at birds or something.

Great. I probably had a concussion. The pain in my cheekbones and jaw was almost unbearable. I had to think of something fast.

"Wait!" I said as Jack reared his arm for another punch. "Okay, okay, you win. I've got wads of cash here in my bag. I'll give all of it to you."

As expected, Jack let go immediately, the rage in his eyes dampened with greed. He gave me a small, impatient nod. I put my backpack on the bench and pretended to rummage inside the pockets while searching for the one thing I needed.

"Right inside here, you see," I said, pointing to the open backpack with a sigh of relief. "Mind helping me check? I'm sure I left twenties in here."

I lifted my open bag to his face. Jack, curious and stupid, peered in. His head dipped further. This was my chance to escape. I reached behind his head, grabbed his neck, and slammed his face against the metal binders. A satisfying crunch followed. Jack screamed. With one swift roundhouse kick, I managed to get him to double over and sink to his knees.

Kyle swung out a hand, trying to grab me. I ducked

out of the way, snatched up my bag and phone, and took off with Zachary on my heels.

I leaped over the stroller as the mother swerved it out of my way just in time. I caught her glower and the squealing toddler clapping and waving in delight. Another surge of energy coursed through me. Boy, did it feel good to fight back. Just like old times.

I wiped my nose, ignoring the blood. In my adrenaline-fueled state, I barely registered the pain. I ran out of the park, heading toward the city's crowded streets. The few flickers of horror and disgust I saw on the people told me I looked bad enough. Their horror turned to surprise as their gazes flew past me. I knew then that Zachary, with his athletic build, was catching up to me fast.

In an open space, Zachary would have grabbed me already. But, as I wriggled my way through the growing crowd of people, I had one advantage over him. It felt good for once to know the city better than anyone. Move quickly while staying low—a lesson I'd learned years ago. A quick glance over my shoulder told me Zachary had slowed his pace, struggling to get past everyone. I kept my head down and then pushed past a few people at a medium speed.

The good news was that I could now safely get home. A hand suddenly grabbed my shirt. I spun around, fists up, to find a child reaching out to me, watching my bloody

AJ DASHER & KRIS RUHLER

face with curious eyes. Darn, I nearly hit the small guy. I blew out a sigh of relief. *Stop being paranoid.*

I briefly checked my watch. Janet and Mark were about to set off, and I suddenly really wanted to see them. A strange dread built up inside me. I trusted my instincts, and they were urging me to get back home at this very moment.

Lately, I'd been shrugging off Janet's hugs, knowing full well my attitude hurt her. I'd mumble at Mark if he'd ask me anything. I didn't know why until now. I thought I was just angry about the stupid trip. But I was really afraid of being without them. Of them abandoning me, even if it was just for ten days. They'd saved me from life on the streets, and I didn't want to go back.

I was scared of losing them and being on my own again.

Life was already hard at fourteen.

I glanced around. No sign of Jack, Kyle, or Zachary. I made my way through the crowd and headed back home.

I rounded the last corner when I caught a glimpse of a red bandanna over auburn hair. I ducked behind a bush, cringing at the thought that such a tiny thing could easily hide my lanky frame. On the bright side, I could keep my head low.

Jack was relentless. He knew where I lived. What he didn't know was that I'd be alone for the next ten days. Maybe I should skip school for the next four days before the break. Not that I'd miss much—other than my favorite science classes. Even the teachers looked like they needed a much-deserved break.

My heart pounded as I retraced my steps back to the crowd, ignoring the incoming messages from my phone. I couldn't stop the guilt gnawing away my insides. Janet deserved better than that. I retrieved my phone and typed a quick 'Sorry. Will try to be back soon' before moving away.

An eerie feeling came over me, and I ducked behind an empty trashcan. And just in time, too. The trio came around the corner like a pack of predators sniffing for prey.

I was cornered, with a wall behind me and piles of trash cans not big enough to hide behind.

"I saw his fricking head just now. Where'd he go?" Jack's head whipped back and forth, a bloody piece of cloth hanging from his nose. I gave myself a mental high-five. I did a good job with that slam to his head. The metal binder did the rest.

"Let's go back to his house," Zachary suggested.

Unlike Kyle, who could be nice at times, and Jack, who had no brain at all, Zachary had half a brain and could keep up with the chase. "Sooner or later, he's got to go home. We'll catch him then."

I waited for them to move away, but to my dismay, Zachary suddenly moved closer, peering at the space between the trashcans. Darn it, why wasn't he born without a brain?

I had to do something before they found me. So, I swung my backpack into Zachary's face, causing him to fall onto his back. Then, I kicked the garbage can toward Jack, who doubled over and bolted away from Kyle before he could make a move. It took a while before I heard their steps thumping behind me. I risked a glance behind me. Zachary was hot on my heels, a hand on his jaw.

The chase was on again.

CHAPTER 4

This city area was unfamiliar, even though I knew the west end of Golden Birch better than my three pursuers. Weaving through the street corners and the crowd, I ditched them again. I cut through an alley and dodged a puddle from which a foul smell wafted. I dived away, disgusted, when I suddenly froze.

A tall, abandoned building stood before me.

It was at least thirty stories high, I evaluated. Then, it hit me why it looked familiar. Westview Hospital was on the news and even made headlines. Once a renowned hospital, the building was now just a dilapidated structure and abandoned for multiple reasons, most suspicious. The building leaned at an unnatural angle, like the Tower of Pisa.

In my books, it was as good a hiding place as any. Still, I hesitated. The rumors of horrible experiments and strange disappearances were fresh in my mind. Some said it was just a made-up story.

But rumors were just rumors. It was either hide inside this crumbling structure or face a bloody beating. I ducked behind the yellow warning tape and burst through the building's entrance door. Of course, it was unlocked. Despite the stuffy smell and debris, the stairs looked sturdy enough, so I scrambled up. On the third floor, I stopped by the window and peeked to see where the tyrants were.

Wrong move.

"I see him! He's in there!" Zachary's muffled voice called out. He pointed at me.

Dammit. I didn't wait. I rushed up the stairs again and kept climbing until I ran out of breath. A step cracked under my weight, but I was too fast. Perhaps Jack's foot might plunge through. Gasping for breath, I stopped at an exit door and twisted the handle. It was locked. I didn't bother checking the other doors and went back to climbing the stairwell.

Soon enough, Jack's voice echoed up the stairway. "Let's get him, guys. No one beats us and gets away with it! Move faster! You're in my way!"

I'd like to remind Jack that he got beaten by skinny Alex this morning. I remembered his widened eyes and the shock on his face. How Alex caused that, I'd never know. Either way, I'd humiliated Jack one too many times in front of his goons, and he'd never give up on the chase.

The sound of their steps went from creaking to cracking. The ground under my sneakers sank like quicksand. I had to stop. I didn't know much about engineering, but the surface of the upper floors seemed to be crumbling from the damage caused by the sinkhole. A few floors up, I jumped off a broken stair and exited the stairway to find a good hiding place.

Wouldn't that be ironic? Chased by bullies, running to escape their wrath, only to fall to my death. Death by irony.

A dark, fuzzy silhouette appeared at the end of the corridor, startling me. My heart skipped several beats. The silhouette framed by the setting sun grew larger. It shivered, and only then did I realize it was a cat. Of course, it wasn't afraid of abandoned, deadly buildings. It had nine lives, after all. I only had one that I was desperately clinging to.

Behind the cat was the front façade of the building, which collapsed to a bunch of rubble, allowing the warm rays of the setting sun to stream in. A few support beams were placed at intervals. The floor was cleared, the walls empty, and any equipment that might've once existed here was removed.

What terrible luck. I had nowhere to hide. The entire city of Golden Birch sprawled out before me. My high school looked like a smudge in the distance, my house a tiny dot. As I looked around frantically, the door to the stairway slammed open. Jack and the other two bullies stalked through.

I stepped back involuntarily and then reassessed. Behind me, there was nothing but a plunge to my death. Just a big yawning gap with no safety rails. No way could I get past the three guys. I was trapped. Again. Except this time, I wasn't sure how to escape.

Jack had a wide smile plastered across his face. "You shouldn't have done that to my face, little Mikey. There's nowhere for you to run now. You know better than me that actions got consequences. We got to even this out. So, how about it then? Stop running, and we'll call it a day." He cracked his knuckles.

Beneath his snigger and confident words, Jack looked weary from the chase. I could tell he wanted this to be over. But he'd never let go of this. He had to save face and make me pay for the humiliation. Thoughts swirled through my mind. How was I supposed to defend myself? I picked up a small chunk of brick from the debris scattered around.

"You gonna throw that at me?" Jack said, a challenge in his voice. "Here I am, doing my best to show mercy, trying to forget that ball you threw at my face. Man, that hurt, you know? And now you're just being ungrateful!"

"Well, you should've caught it. You're the sports guy."

To be honest, I couldn't remember *throwing* the ball in his face. The ball went to his face of its own...will? Maybe his face was just *that* dislikable.

"You think you're really smart, don't you?" Jack went on. "I heard you in science class. Think you're better than me?" He bent down and picked up a stone. One which was easily three times as big as mine.

My breath caught in my throat as I saw him flex his arm back. Then he flung it in my direction as if it weighed nothing. I flinched, my feet frozen on the spot, but phew! Luckily for me—him being the sports guy and all—the stone flew way past me to my right. He really must be tired from the chase.

Kyle and Zachary followed suit, picking up a stone each and rearing their arms back, ready to throw.

I swallowed hard and took a hesitant step back, raising my arms in defense. "Jack, come on, man," I said. "Don't do this. I didn't throw that ball. I swear. And you know how Mr. Hoffmann is such a terrible teacher and gets annoyed so quickly, right? I couldn't give him the wrong answer, okay?"

My plea didn't seem to work. Instead, Jack's face flushed a worrying reddish tint. *You idiot, why'd you go and remind him you had the right answer and he had the wrong one?*

Kyle hurled his rock at me. Half-heartedly. I dodged

it easily. Unfortunately, I found myself closer to the edge. Zachary had a good throw, one that I didn't see coming. As if in slow motion, I watched the rock sail straight at my face. My hands lifted to shield myself from the onslaught.

A red barrier burst out from nowhere, and Zachary's rock bounced back right at him, knocking him on the shoulder. The rebound was so powerful that Zachary fell backward on his bottom. Again. He got back to his feet, groaning with a hand clutching his shoulder.

Jack was now moving closer, holding another piece of debris. Part of me actually wanted to move forward and let him beat me up. That part of me that knew I couldn't keep dodging like this. Yet another part of me didn't want to give up. I had no idea where that red barrier had come from, but there was no time to dwell on it.

Nose smudged in dried blood, Jack reared his arm back again, and I braced myself, lifting my hands up. They felt like they were on fire, but the adrenaline coursing through me made it easy to ignore the pain. Another red barrier appeared from nowhere between my hands, and the heavy rock bounced back. Again.

My eyes widened, and I stared at the waves of energy emanating from between my hands. Like a glass platform, the barrier looked like the waves of heat radiating from a road on a hot day, tinted crimson. I moved my hands, and the red energy bolts arced back and forth through the glass. I shook them again, and the glass platform wavered in sync.

I frowned. That platform defied every law of gravity and…pretty much everything scientific. The look on Jack and Kyle's faces mimicked my confusion. Zachary edged closer to the exit to the stairs, ready to bolt. For a moment, I forgot that the imminent menace was Jack.

"What the—? How did you hit—? What the hell are you looking at, anyway? You some kind of freak?" Jack scowled. "I don't know what tricks you're up to, so how about we agree on five punches, and we'll call it even? Ain't that right, boys?"

So only I could see this strange red glass platform. And before I could gather my thoughts, the red waves were gone just as quickly as they'd appeared.

Kyle's head lowered as his eyes shifted sideways. If I was reading him right, Jack was in his usual unhinged mood, his eyes raving mad. No way could I trust him with his dumb five-punch deal.

"Jack, just let it go. We're really high up—" Kyle started.

Jack threw him a dagger-like glare. "Shut up!" he shouted.

Shaking his head, Kyle started to inch away, too, toward the exit where Zachary stood.

"Come on, little Mikey," Jack continued, his voice dangerously low. "We just want to play, and it'll all be over."

The orange sun glared behind me, but it wasn't bright enough to blind Jack. A soft click echoed around us. A flash caught my eye.

A blade, poorly hidden behind his back.

Dread pooled inside me like ice in my veins. I now understood why even Kyle was moving away. Jack stepped closer. The clicking sounds told me he was flicking his pen knife back and forth. At least, I assumed it was a pen knife. My eyes were locked with Jack's, and I couldn't look away.

"I don't want trouble," I said, hating my shaky voice. "Just don't hurt me. I have money at home. I'll get you some, I promise."

Jack shrugged, and my heart sank. "Come on, little Mikey, back away from the ledge. We just want to have a little chat. Don't make me come and get you. I promise you if I do, it'll be much, much worse."

In hindsight, yeah, I should've listened to him. It did get much worse after that.

What came next was totally unexpected. It went down so fast, yet it was as if I was watching it in slow motion.

I backpedaled without realizing it. So, the edge of the tenth-floor front façade was a mere five paces away. A cool breeze brushed against the back of my neck, sending a shiver running down my spine.

As I stood in a defensive stance, one foot in front of another, I came to realize that not only was the floor slightly slanted, but there was a thin coat of ice under my boots.

My heels pressed hard against the floor, my whole body tense at the thought of the ledge behind me. A ledge that shielded me from a sixty-foot-long fall. Jack kept flicking his pen knife, the sound grating on my nerves.

Surprisingly, it was Kyle who made the first move. He lunged at Jack, grabbing the hand holding the pen knife, startling me. I staggered backward... It wasn't entirely Kyle's fault; it had only been my body responding involuntarily, a reflexive action.

Suddenly, a gust flew by, whistling through the empty floor and cracked columns, making my legs even more unsteady. My arms pinwheeled, reaching for a handhold that wasn't there. Before I could move, an unnatural growl like a lion echoed from far below me. Weird. But there was no time to contemplate that. My hands reached out, desperate to hold on to something. Anything.

Kyle and Jack's eyes widened as they stared at me flapping about. Zachary didn't stick around to see what would happen. He bolted through the exit, and the door slammed behind him, the boom echoing around me. That was the final push.

The floor rose slightly before me, and the room spun. Correction: it was me losing balance as my boots slipped and the floor dipped further behind me.

You could say that the stupidest reaction was me waving and dangling about. My brain should've picked up quickly on the fact that I was slipping far too quickly. I'd been too distracted by my fear of Jack and his knife, and now it was too late. The building's front façade and the edge were close to my back.

My feet slid off the ledge, a high-pitched cry escaped my lips, and my body spun around. Arms wide, I must've looked like I was embracing the entire city of Golden Birch.

That was when I fell to my death, facing the gaping mouth of a sinkhole.

But I wasn't dead. Nor did I hit the ground.

The ground shot up at me still but at a slower rate. I squeezed my eyes shut.

A breeze caressed my arms, and I pried my eyes open. I was floating right above the dark hole, my arms spread wide. Two red pinpoints of light stared back at me, and a distant growling echoed. I'd heard the sound in my dreams so many times that I wasn't even surprised. Just as suddenly as they appeared, the lights vanished.

I held my breath. Between me and the ground was the glass platform. Red crackles of energy flew under me. I should be electrocuted, the logical part of my brain deduced, but the sparks, once again, were harmless. And just like this morning, my energy level surged. I watched the waves rippling across the air for a long time, mesmerized like a kitten with a ball.

Then, my rational mind took over. *Get away before the No-Brains find you again.*

I scooted to the side over the tarmac and did a quick roll, landing on the hard ground. The glass platform disappeared. I stayed still for a long time, watching the top of the building that looked like a dot.

Slowly, I got up to my feet. In the distance, I heard Jack arguing with the guys. I couldn't care less. I now had a much bigger problem. Even as my body felt light and invigorated and the shock was slowly dissipating, everything hurt: my legs, arms, back, shoulders, lungs, head.

But I had to move. I had to get back home.

So I dragged my feet along. One step after another. My phone vibrated from inside my backpack. It must be Janet again; I guessed it was well past six. As I rounded the corner to my street, a taxi drove past. I'd just missed them.

I didn't have the energy to wave. I stopped, retrieved my phone, and checked all my missed messages. Two were from Mark. Vaguely surprising since he had an aversion to texting. To my surprise, I forgot all about the pain.

I quickly typed a comforting, well-wishing message for their holiday break. I'd have liked so much to see them before they set off. But they'd be back in ten days. The days would fly by, and everything would be fine, right? Yet, for some reason I couldn't understand, my throat was all tight, and my eyes stung.

It's the shock. My brain couldn't make sense of anything that had happened today. Too many weird things.

In the back of my mind, I knew for sure that my life had changed. Just how much, and whether it was for the better or worse, remained to be seen. That strange instinct—a sense of foreboding—that always nagged at me, warning me of dangers ahead, was right there in my chest and the back of my neck.

The last message was from Katie, the babysitter, and I ignored it. I locked the front door behind me, staggered up the stairs, and got to my room.

I had a quick wash and flopped onto my bed as if on auto mode. As I lay there, staring at the ceiling and waiting for some semblance of sleep, the memory of a pair of red eyes came back to me. Eyes that stared from deep inside the sinkhole. To add to everything else, was I now hallucinating?

Nothing made sense, and my mind was too tired. I drifted into a deep, chaotic sleep.

CHAPTER 5

Day 2

I knew it was a dream, one in which I was a mere spectator. But my heart pounded, and my fear felt so real that I couldn't be entirely sure.

At first, there was the nerve-wracking sound of Jack's pen knife flicking in and out. Then that horrible cat appeared. Instead of meowing like a normal cat, it started growling. Red flashes emitted from its eyes as it started to morph...into a dragon? Orange cloaks flickered in and out of the corner of my eye. Tattooed faces. And they all stood ready to pounce on...Allegra?

I woke up drenched in sweat and my heart racing. The dream had been so vivid. I was the only one who stood between these strange men, the strange monster cat, and Allegra.

I took a deep breath. My mind had probably mixed up the scenes from the multitude of disasters yesterday that happened the day before. The whole day felt unreal. I guessed the monster-dragon in my dream must have been Jack. The thought brought a grimace to my face. Yeah. Accurate enough.

A growl startled me, and I nearly fell out of bed. Darn, I was so jumpy. A stabbing sensation in my mid-section followed, bringing me back to reality. Hunger pangs. Ah, yes, I skipped dinner last night in my rush to collapse and pass out in bed.

It slowly dawned on me that I was home alone, and no syrupy, buttery waffles awaited me downstairs in the kitchen. No Mark or Janet to say good morning. I pushed the thought away and checked my messages. Nothing.

Time to get busy. My hunger pangs were getting worse. And yes, they sounded like an animal growling. They weren't going to go away on their own.

This was enough motivation to drag myself out of bed, albeit slowly. I was in such unbearable pain last night, and I was expecting muscle aches, bruising pains, and stinging cuts. But as I straightened up, my body felt great—other than the hunger pangs, that is.

How strange. In the bathroom, I examined my hands. No tingling. No red sparks or barriers. Next, I inspected my face. Jack had punched me on the jaw and cheek, and I'd literally been slammed into a pole, but no purple bruises marred my skin. Nor was there any pain.

Doubt crept into my mind. Had I somehow imagined a whole afternoon being chased and tortured by the No-Brains trio? Had I really fallen from Westview Hospital? Or was it just a dream I had?

Then, I noticed an odd smudge on the back of my right hand. Washing and scrubbing didn't take it off. Come to think of it, the smudge looked more like a tattoo poorly done. Under the dim bathroom light, I distinguished darker lines: a circle with a shape inside, its vertices connected to the perimeter. Any other lines were too blurry to make out. Yet, the shape was a perfect circle.

Had I landed on something yesterday that had caused the imprint? What the heck? Something clicked in the back of my brain, like a familiar itch that wouldn't leave.

Maybe this strange bruise would wear off in a day or two. A throbbing pain started at my temples, and my vision flashed red for a split second. How could that weird mark feel familiar when I'd never seen it in my life?

I sighed and took a cold shower to lighten the fog in my head. Everything was changing. But first, I needed fuel, a good breakfast.

In a matter of minutes, I was sitting at the breakfast counter, munching on a stack of toast. The silence in the kitchen helped me focus on my train of thought. Still, I missed having Janet fussing around with my orange juice and Mark trailing back and forth with his cup of coffee, reading the news on his tablet. Maybe focusing on my daily goals would help get rid of this feeling of loneliness.

Isn't that what you wanted? Isn't that why you try to be invisible in school? I wanted to stay out of trouble, but now that meant I had no friends and no one to talk to. Yesterday morning at the courtyard was the first time I stood up for myself—or someone else—since I was seven. The kids at the orphanage used to band together and protect each other. It felt good to do it again, rather than the quiet, passive boy I'd tried to be in the last seven years. Still...it wasn't enough. The loneliness hung around the kitchen like a dark fog.

By the time I finished my plate and felt full, I came to several decisions. First, I resolved to show up at school. I needed to know that the events from yesterday had really happened (a cat growling like a lion and morphing into a dragon was supposedly a very real thing that could totally happen).

I flinched at the thought of confronting Jack and the others. Going to school would give me a sense of normalcy—relatively, that is—rather than staying home alone in a practically silent house. And then, of course, there was the matter of the wavy, glassy platform that somehow burst from my hands, assuming yesterday's fall had really happened. Perhaps since these red sparks manifested in the presence of the three bullies, maybe they would again. I had to find out.

Manifested. Now, that was a superhero word. What next? With great power comes great responsibility? Ugh. Great pain more likely. Call me a superhero fan. Shame I couldn't blast webs from my wrist.

Plus, going to school meant I'd have another chance to meet Allegra. Hopefully, without her awful sister throwing dagger-like glares at me this time.

Considering the amount of food I'd just ingested for breakfast, I came to another decision. I cringed, looking at the two empty dinner containers Janet had packed, the half-empty juice carton, the lonely single bite of waffle left over from yesterday, the crumbs from the three slices of toast I was still picking at and munching on, and the jam and syrup spills I'd created in the process of eating.

The tally filled me with awe. And concern. Skipping one dinner wasn't good enough of an excuse for binge eating. Was my metabolism always this insane? Maybe I should start budgeting and rationing for the next nine days. At this rate of ingestion, I would run out of food so on.

Before the orphanage, I went without meals for days at a time and drank from public fountains. After that, I had regular, small meals. Janet and Mark always had more than enough. In fact, Janet would always push me gently to eat a bit more, worried about my thin frame.

I wished she were there to see the kitchen table now.

I quickly tidied and washed up the dishes. I wanted to prove to my foster parents that I was responsible enough. Which was yet another reason to not skip school.

As I grabbed my backpack and ran for the school bus, I mentally counted my lunch money and evaluated the food stock—a couple of hundred-dollar bills for ten dinners and a few snacks in the cupboards. I needed to find some way of making the most of my budget while satiating my appetite. The only method I could think of was buying high-calorie foods like nuts and bars instead of the salads I intended to.

Maybe that sudden hunger had nothing to do with the, uh, red-spark thingy shooting from my hands. Maybe I was just going through a growth spurt. Too bad I was left alone to fend for myself at the wrong time. Not that I'd even be able to explain this to anyone.

In the school courtyard, I searched frantically for dark, wavy hair and hazel eyes. Instead, I found Jack and Zachary in the courtyard, sitting on a bench in silence with distant gazes. No sniggering, no gossiping, no scrawny boy around for them to pick on. I hesitated to pass by them, but before I could retreat, Jack's gaze fell on me.

He froze. I froze, too. His elbows rested on his legs as he leaned forward, hands clasped in apparent contemplation. Zachary was sitting back and staring at the sky, oblivious of my appearance.

Jack and I stared at each other for a long time. I wasn't looking forward to another beating; to my dismay, no red waves appeared between my hands.

My theory that a meeting with the No-Brains trio would trigger the red-spark-thingy just went bust. Getting closer to the two didn't make any difference, either.

Jack's head tipped to one side, frowning. "Thought I gave you a black eye."

"Guess I don't bruise easily, or your punches don't work on me." I recalled the excruciating pain and stars in my vision when my head whipped back. His punches worked great for sure, but if I bluffed my way out of this, maybe he'd leave me alone. Or he'd get annoyed and give me another black eye.

To my surprise, he turned away, avoiding my eyes. Zachary turned away, too. In shame or disgust or fear, I didn't know.

"What do you want?" Jack said.

"Uh, I was just walking past." I pointed to the water fountain. "Where's your buddy Kyle?"

Jack's shoulders slumped, an uneasy look on his face.

"Somewhere," he said, "I'll tell him you're...alive, I guess. We all saw you fall off that building, you know." He stopped, waiting for an explanation. I didn't have any.

I understood then. "Kyle went to report you."

"Well, you're fricking alive and well, aren't you? So it doesn't matter."

"Yet I fell off the building, right? You all saw me."

Jack's silence told me he was evaluating the consequences of his actions. Well, if I'd been found dead, that is.

"What would've happened if I'd died, huh?" I continued relentlessly. "You'd get another slap on the wrist like all the times you bullied other people? You really think you'd have gotten away with it? Your father owns this school and the teachers. Does he own the law, too?"

"Shut up! It's not like any of us pushed you! You just...you just slipped!"

I shrugged. "I wouldn't have been in that building in the first place if it weren't for you. You'd have killed an innocent kid. Not a good look, Jack."

His face morphed into a mixture of primal horror and rage. "I said, shut up!" His lip trembled ever so slightly with the words.

Perhaps I went too far. I took a step back as nonchalantly as I could.

"You think anyone will take Kyle's word or yours over mine?" Jack said, clenching his fists, spittle flying. "Think again!"

"There were a few witnesses in that park. And for once in your life, think for a moment. I stopped those rocks, Jack. Heck, in gym class, I shoved that ball into your face. With. Just. A. Thought. So, yeah. Think about that next time you bully someone else."

I took another step back. Then, just for effect, I lunged forward with my palms facing forward. To my delight, Jack recoiled, fear in his eyes. A high-pitched shriek spilled from his lips. I couldn't help the smile that spread across my lips. I tried to bite back the laugh bubbling inside and maintained what I hoped was an evil look in my gaze. Jack scooted closer to Zachary.

A little bit of shame coursed through me. Having people fear me wasn't a particularly nice feeling. I could only hope that with this, Jack's bullying days were over. Zachary and Kyle's, too.

The bell rang, and Jack's shoulders sagged with relief. As I got in line to the school's entrance door, my gaze unexpectedly met Allegra's. I blinked, realizing I never truly looked into her eyes. In class, it was always her profile. In the corridor, she always had her eyes lowered. Now, looking deep into her hazel eyes practically took my breath away.

My mouth opened to say hello. Or hi. Damn, I had once rehearsed a witty speech in a daydream, but now, my mind was blank. No words came out. Her hands lifted hesitantly toward me as if in slow motion, and her lips stretched into a small smile. Her lips moved, uttering words I couldn't hear.

Then, the moment broke. A scowling face planted itself between us. Alex. Her murderous gaze, hazel eyes so similar to her sister's, made me duck away and head toward my science class, thoughts swirling in my head.

Part of me fumed with anger. How could I ever hope to talk to the girl I liked without her sister getting all up in my face? Then there was my dream. I was willing to die in it to protect that girl from bald men and cat monsters. A girl I barely knew—well, one that I was *dying* to know, anyway. Actually, recounting the dream like that made it sound even weirder than it already was. What the heck.

And dang, how could the twins be so different when they looked the same? One was always frowning and angry, while the other made my heart skip a beat with just one look.

Then the treacherous part of me wondered: was Allegra really Jack's girlfriend? I know that, with Jack's connections, good looks, and athletic build, many girls swooned around him.

The thought made me feel dejected. Not only did my glassy-platform superpower fail to manifest, but now, I might have no chance at all with Allegra. I thought that in English class, she'd come and talk to me since she smiled at me, but my hopes were dashed. She didn't even glance at me as she followed her sister in and out of class.

All day, I searched for wavy, dark hair and hazel eyes. I would've liked so much to be able to talk to her. Well, without Alex around.

While mulling it over, I came up with another theory about the thing that appeared between my hands. It was some kind of shield. Which made sense since it protected me from the ball and the stones the bullies were throwing at me.

This shield seemed to appear when I was under attack, right? It also helped to cushion my fall. So, a protective shield, I'd call it. Maybe it was my line of defense.

So before the actual danger appeared, aka the No-Brains, the tingling feeling and my sixth sense warned me.

All I needed for this red protective shield to appear again was to put myself in danger. It was simple enough, I thought.

CHAPTER 6

As I pondered over the issue, I realized it wasn't simple at all. Without Jack, being in danger was a hard thing to accomplish, and heck, how did one get into trouble? Like in real mortal danger? Not to mention the fact that this was pretty much counterintuitive to, like, some of my most basic survival instincts. I was not about to throw myself from another building to test my shield theories.

In fact, the government kept telling us it was all good and there wasn't much trouble in the whole world. A few countries posed a threat, missiles and stuff, and that was it. Just threats and nothing more. When some higher-ups lowered the age for compulsory schooling to the age of seven, nobody protested (I was glad Janet chose to send me to school). Heck, when the same higher-ups took away the right to protest, well, nobody protested. With the fear of floods, heatwaves, and calamities running rampant, the focus had been on rebuilding and, basically, survival.

After school, I made my way toward the deserted courtyard. No one was expecting me home (yep, the thought was crushing instead of elating), so I thought of ambling around till dinner. The last week before the break was usually boring, so I had little else to do. No tests to study for, no homework, and no friends to hang out with.

But I had a challenge to contend with, something interesting that defied any scientific explanations. How could I make this shield appear again? I shook my hands. Nope.

Time to test that theory of being in danger. I braced myself and ran straight into the outside wall.

Ouch. That hurt bad. I looked at my hands. My heart sank; it didn't work.

"That wall must have really ticked you off," a soft voice said, startling me.

When I turned around, my heart skipped a beat. Allegra stood before me with a raised eyebrow. Ah, yes, the running-into-a-wall move. Not smart at all. I recovered quickly. I'd been looking for an opportunity to talk to her all day, and here she was.

"Yeah, just practicing." Lame and pathetic. Who threw themselves at a wall for practice? Practicing what? Pain management? (Huh, now that I thought of it, maybe that actually made sense.)

She didn't look convinced. She glanced behind her, most likely checking for an overprotective Alex.

"I just wanted to say thanks," she continued hurriedly, "For, um, yesterday. Standing up to Jack like that. I heard they were watching out for you in the afternoon near the bus. I looked for you to try to warn—I was worried, but I'm glad you're alright." She spoke in a rush. Maybe the trailing accent made her words stumble into each other.

"I'm fine," I said, cringing at the remembrance of yesterday's fall off the building. "They just—"

I stopped mid-sentence as the realization dawned on me. She heard they were looking for me? That was strange.

"Where'd you hear that?"

She blinked. "What?"

"Where'd you hear that they were waiting for me?"

"Uh, someone must've said something. Gossip, you know?" She looked a little panicked, I noticed, her eyes darting around. Obviously, she had a secret she didn't want to share, so I just nodded and changed the subject.

"Hey, you know that waffle place at the mall?" I said. She nodded. "Maybe we could go there some time? Whenever you're okay with it…"

Her face beamed, and I relaxed. "I'd love that! I'll have to—Oh, but I'm not allowed to go anywhere." Just then, steps thudded in our direction. "Hide!"

Instinctively, I moved away and crouched down behind a bench. Alex turned up and admonished sweet Allegra for disappearing on her. Blah, blah, blah. Allegra's tone was meek, yet the defiance underneath was plain. Could it be that it was obvious only to me? It was as if I'd known her for a long time.

I sighed in relief when both girls moved away. It was a long while before I got up. By then, I decided to make my next move and head to the more crowded areas of Golden Birch.

More specifically, I headed for the west end, toward the thirty-story building: Westview Hospital. Reckless as it might be, it was time to put my theory to the test.

I had no death wish. But the west end of our city was the most dangerous, with clubs and bars open all day and night, dark alleyways, and notorious gang members patrolling the neighborhood. In this part of the city, dilapidated shops, graffiti, leaky pipes, and rusty cars were a common sight. Even the patrol drones didn't venture there after so many had been shot down.

One thing I knew about these gangs was that one wrong look could get you killed. All I had to do was find trouble and then run from it. Easy, right?

As I walked down the streets and moved further away from the city's center, keeping my eyes and chin up took some effort. Just the day before, I had rushed through the same streets. Being chased in full daylight was a normal sight. Maybe that was why nobody came to my help.

This time, I had time to study the brightly lit shop fronts, the cars with no license plates, and the different groups of people hanging around. Gang members didn't like nosy people. It didn't take long to catch someone's attention. At first, they just threw me a nasty look. My hands tingled, and my breath hitched like a weight settled on my chest.

Suddenly, a small red wave radiated from my palms. A red spark followed, zipping from one finger to another. There it was. Elated that the red waves had appeared again, I flexed my fingers. The tingling sensation felt like my fingers fell asleep. I relaxed my hands, realizing I wasn't entirely sure how it worked yet. What if a sudden movement created a shield out of nowhere? Who knew if it would knock a bird or an insect in flight? Or hit one of the gang members?

I could barely contain my excitement. My theory was right: when my sixth sense detected danger close by, the red waves formed, circling my fingers.

Could I form any shape or only a rectangle? Was the shield malleable? I knew that it could make a cushiony platform. But right now, it looked like a translucent rubber band that could wrap around my arms, maybe.

What if I threw the band around an attacker? Was

this sixth sense precognitive? Could I sense the future? I needed to do more research and resolved to write everything down, cataloging each discovery. I needed to fully explore this newfound ability. But how could I practice?

Lost in my thoughts, it took a long time for me to fully realize the extent of my discovery. I froze on the spot, the rubber band ceasing its movement too.

Danger was close by. *You moron.*

A pair of sneakers squeaked behind me—how ironic that sneakers never actually let you sneak behind someone. I stopped and crouched down, pretending to tie my laces. The footsteps stopped, too. I swallowed my panic. I could defend myself, right? I crossed two junctions, increasing my pace. The footsteps picked up their pace, too.

I considered darting into an alleyway and facing my pursuers head-on. At the third crossroad, three sets of soft footsteps sounded behind me. I risked a glance over my shoulder. Three teens wearing black caps and sunglasses. I knew exactly what they were thinking: skinny kid with a backpack, easy prey, easy money off his sneakers, jacket, and everything they could resell.

Also, what was with bullies traveling in packs of three? Was there some unspoken, cosmic bully harmony in the number three? Was this a hivemind thing?

Something surged inside me, a need to face them,

to show them I wasn't afraid. Not after yesterday's near-death experience.

I looked up. Westview Hospital, the crumbling building, stood before me. My heart sank. It was almost like my steps had brought me back to this place. I wasn't even conscious that I was heading toward it.

Further to my right were orange cones, warning barriers around the sinkhole. When my gaze met the leaning façade where I fell toward the sinkhole, I turned away, ducking under the yellow tape, my heart pounding.

I hid behind a rickety wall and waited. No footsteps followed. Yet, when I lifted my hands, the waves remained. In fact, the shield was growing, and the surrounding view rippled. I was pretty certain no one could see the waves or the red crackles of electricity coursing the net-like shield, so it didn't bother me. Still, I remained still and waited. Could I really relax when even those three teens seemed to avoid this awful place?

After a while, I rounded the corner to a backyard and leaned against a pile of debris. Maybe testing that theory again wasn't a good idea. Putting myself in trouble was far too nerve-wracking.

The waves didn't retreat. But no one was around; I was certain of it.

Oh yeah, I was around the knockoff leaning Tower of Pisa that could come crashing down on my head any minute.

I looked around the deserted backyard. No better place to test things out with that shield like I wanted to, right? I stretched my hands to each side as if holding a giant board and flicked my wrist. The glassy platform expanded and hit a pile of debris about ten paces away. A few stones scattered from the ridge.

This is so cool.

A hum sounded. As I drew my hands closer together, the platform, like elastic, would stretch back into a smaller shape. Excitement filled me. The shield was rigid one moment and flexible the next. I could play with this thing for hours.

Calling it a shield was a good idea, I figured. It deserved respect. It protected me from rocks and being slammed in the gym by a ball. A few moments later, I discovered I could thin the shield into a rope lasso and latch it onto a boulder. I could even morph it into a blanket and wrap it around the entire thing.

I was drained by the time the sun was sinking low in the sky, so I decided to head home. Going through the west end at nighttime was no big deal, right? Surprisingly enough, the walk home was uneventful.

A chilly breeze blew around me, and the clouds above were grey and looking rather ominous, but no one paid me much attention, too absorbed in the nightlife.

As I shrugged my backpack higher on my shoulders and made my way back home, my heart fluttered in triumph. For the first time in a while, I felt strong.

CHAPTER 7

Day 3

You know that sense of dread after a nightmare? That's exactly how I felt when I woke up, my heart pounding. I got home the previous night just before the storm hit. I listened for a while, but outside my window, everything seemed normal. Yet, something was amiss.

I looked down at my hands. In the morning light, a red haze swirled around them.

My first thought was: robbers. I crept downstairs in my pajamas, barefoot. Holding on to a wooden paddle I carved in woodwork class last semester, I crouched behind the living room sofa and waited.

Something else sent me on edge, and I had to think fast. Firstly, there was danger. This shield stuff was proof of that. I tried to recall my dream.

A child in a stroller giving me a thumbs-up. Right. Very helpful, memory.

That was in the park while the bullies chased me. So, I concluded that the danger might not be close by.

I couldn't be sure, though. Beastly hunger pangs gnawed at my stomach. They were worse than the previous day and I was sure they were linked to my shield now. It seemed the more I practiced, the more energy my body demanded. I needed food.

I quickly came to a decision. It was as if my body and these red swirly things knew something was about to happen, even when I didn't have any clue. I had to trust my instincts. And right now, they told me most likely there wasn't a robber and that I should head to Broadway Park.

I ran upstairs and changed quickly. The mark on the back of my right hand was no longer a smudge. The dark lines were sharper, like a tattoo: a triangle within a circle that contained an 'X' shape. As I looked closer, the 'X' had a black dot where the lines intersected in the middle.

After a quick wash, I grabbed my backpack, emptied it on the floor, and tossed in a bottle of juice and several bars. I'd fix myself a good breakfast later. With that in mind, I was out. Like I thought, no one was around the house. No potential robbers or intruders in sight. Hauling my backpack over my shoulder, I quickened my pace until I was almost running.

The sun was just peeking above the horizon, and the streets were deserted. A few branches were scattered across the roads, and a car drove around them. I must've been in a deep sleep since I didn't hear the wind howling at my window.

As I drew near the park, my sense of dread increased to such a level that my breathing became erratic. I stopped short and took a deep breath.

Unsurprisingly, the red swirls around my wrist turned a shade darker and thickened. Like it was getting ready to burst out and protect me.

Yet, when I looked around, I saw no one.

My usual spot was the bench. But I only took a few steps forward when a shriek broke the silence.

A raven? A sound like a growling hiccup followed. I once heard that sound on a nature show. A hyena. But what was something like that doing in the park?

My heart raced with fear. The sound came from my right, so I veered and made my way over slowly. A strange sensation overcame me as I shielded my eyes against the blinding sun's rays.

As I reached the swings, a billowing flash of orange caught my attention. Blinking, I took two steps forward. It was a cloak. The same two people that I saw the previous morning and thought were stage actors. I recalled they were in my nightmare from the night before, too.

I instinctively hid behind a tree trunk before considering this action. Why should I be scared of stage actors? But something was off about them.

The hyena-like sound echoed again, startling me. Watching a pair of shaking shoulders, I realized the man was laughing.

He turned briefly to check his right side. I followed his gaze and stifled a gasp. Someone lay on the grassy ground. Unconscious or dead, I didn't know. But I'd recognize that spiky brown hair anywhere. If the figure on the ground was Alex, then Allegra couldn't be too far away .

When I turned my gaze back, the man had shifted further to his right as if studying Alex, and that was when I saw Allegra.

Eyes storming with anger, chin raised, and fists clenched, she faced the two men who were well over a foot taller than her. Tension radiated from her, and the air felt electrifying like it was charged. So fearless, I thought. (I had to admit that I was just a little awestruck.)

My next thought was to knock the two men down with the shield while remaining in my hiding spot. But when I looked down at my hands, the red swirls were gone.

Not now! I almost cursed aloud in frustration. *Allegra needs my help!*

Should I throw myself in between them and Allegra? I'd be in danger if I drew closer to the two men. No doubt I'd end up like Alex on the ground.

Think, Michael, think!

But seeing Allegra facing two burly men turned my mind blank. I could barely breathe from the fear. Suddenly, I recalled the strange vibration that swept through me as I crossed the path a few steps away near the swings.

Slowly and staying out of sight, I backed away, keeping my gaze riveted on the men. As I stepped onto the cobblestones, the vibration coursed through me again, and faint swirls appeared around my hands.

A sigh of relief escaped my chest. So, something was blocking my shield. Now that it was back, I waited till it reformed and darkened to the shade of embers.

In fact, I was surprised at the speed at which it responded and molded itself into a lasso. While still keeping out of sight, I lashed out, throwing out the shield like a whip at one of the men.

He groaned aloud and stumbled. I didn't wait. I pulled back the shield and lashed out again, this time at the other man. He staggered and fell to the ground, his hands over his bald head. When he removed them, emitting guttural sounds, bloody streaks marred his skin.

The strange sounds were a foreign language, one I'd never heard before: a combination of hiccups, retching, and hissing. The other man nodded. They both turned toward Alex, who was staggering back to her feet.

Weirdly enough, an abject fear filled both men's eyes

as they exchanged a glance. Then, they both looked down at a silver object in their hands. One clicked the top end of the silver tube several times, blurted out weird sounds again, and finally, both men bolted away, their cloaks rustling as they disappeared from the park.

Why were two grown men so terrified of Alex? Allegra rushed to her sister's side and held onto her arm.

That was my cue to disappear. But then something even weirder happened, and I stopped short.

A dog appeared. It was the same one from the previous morning, the one that Alex and Allegra had mysteriously denied seeing.

Alex crouched down to pick up the leash and something round and shiny like a medal. Then, she started talking to the dog while it held the medal in its jaw and nodded. As if it understood Alex.

"The dog...is real?"

Only when both girls turned toward me did I realize I'd spoken aloud. *Real smart question, Michael.*

"I was just passing, uh, by," I started. "Then I saw these men in golden cloaks. Strange actors, don't you think?" I was flustered and panicking already.

Go away!

The words screamed into my mind, startling me so much that I stepped back, looking around. My gaze flickered over the two girls.

Go away!

Their lips never moved, yet it was Alex's voice in my head. Eyes fierce, hands on her hips, she glared at me.

I couldn't look away, even as I took another step back. Slowly, I ran a hand through my hair. My fingers shook. My lips trembled.

I took another step back, staggered, and almost fell over.

Wait, your hand...

Again, her lips didn't move. A shiver ran down my spine. All I knew was that I had to *go away*.

Away from Allegra.

Away from the dog holding the medal in its jaw and cocking its head to the side.

Away from Alex, whose voice echoed in my mind.

I ran all the way back home. I didn't even check my hands to see what Alex was talking about. As soon as I stepped inside the house and locked the front door behind me, I felt a little more at ease, although my breathing was still uneven.

Making a good breakfast of waffles, syrup, toast, and an egg helped calm my nerves. I sat at the kitchen table and took small bites while letting my thoughts drift.

Amazing how much a bit of food could clear your thoughts. I slowly recapped the events of the past few days in my head.

That voice in my mind terrified me. Who wouldn't be scared, anyway? I then understood why those two men and the bullies feared her.

I'd always kept my thoughts to myself. They were meant to be private. Now I wondered: if Alex could push thoughts into my mind, could she also read them?

She must know my feelings toward Allegra then if that were true. *Dammit.*

Being telepathic was something otherworldly, yes. But so was this red shield that burst from my hands when I needed it. No science could explain these abilities. At least, not yet.

Then, there was that sense of dread that had woken me up this morning. Sure, Allegra was in danger, but the shield wouldn't awaken me every time someone somewhere was in trouble. This meant that the inexplicable connection I felt with Allegra was real.

Lastly, my thoughts veered to the strange two men wearing golden, glittery cloaks. What were they trying to do?

As I cleared all the dishes, I concluded that everything about them was otherworldly. What was the silver object in their hands? I could draw only one conclusion: the silver object was the thing that had blocked my ability. Maybe it had blocked Alex's, too. Was that how they had beaten her?

But the blocking ability was also limited to a certain distance. Which wasn't reassuring at all. If you were about to be attacked, you'd have to see them from at least a hundred meters away.

Now that I was calm and thinking clearly, I checked the time. My next decision was whether to go to school or not. Today was a full day, and tomorrow, Thursday, school ended early.

Did I have the courage to show up there? Just the thought of meeting Alex made my nerves all jittery once more.

After agonizing moments, I got tired of the indecision. I couldn't stay in the house out of fear. Fear of what? It wasn't as if she'd knock me down in front of the whole school. I was becoming paranoid. My sixth sense must be working overtime.

I was really glad that the Jacobs were away. They were safer being far away from here. Janet would've fussed over me, seeing me like this. Besides, where would I even begin to explain any of this? I could barely make heads or tails of it myself.

Yesterday had been all exciting, and now the novelty was fading. All that was left was a tad bit of fear and unease.

I needed my routine. I wanted to feel normal again, sit in Mr. Hoffmann's class, and answer his random pop quizzes. So, I grabbed my backpack and gathered all my books scattered across the floor.

I still wanted to see Allegra. Just the thought of her beaming smile when she thanked me the previous day warmed my heart. I couldn't wait to see her again. She didn't need to know that I hit the two attackers. I wanted no thanks from her.

As I stepped onto the yellow bus, I knew I'd made the right decision. The kids howling at the back, the driver going at breakneck speed, and the jolts and swerves all made me feel normal.

Yeah, everything was good. Things would work out just fine. Who knows, maybe I'd even be lucky enough to meet Allegra again without her sister interfering.

But as the day went by, luck was definitely not on my side. All morning, Allegra didn't even glance toward me in class, and I had zero chances to talk to her.

As I sat in the cafeteria during lunch, my luck got even worse. Instead of Allegra, Alex headed toward me, eyebrows furrowed.

CHAPTER 8

I quickly glanced at my hands. Only a thin, red, smoky line was present. Meh, the fried chips and layer of grease on my tray were probably more of a threat than Alex.

Still, as she drew closer, I couldn't help squirming slightly in discomfort, wishing I could make myself smaller. How could I keep her away from my thoughts—assuming she could read them? I decided to think of a wall and then of a massive black hole in that wall. *Try getting past that.*

Was she about to lecture me about this morning? I was in a public park and had every right to be. What if she thought I was stalking her sister? I could tell her the truth; I woke up, felt scared, thought of the park to relax, and ran straight toward it. Yeah. Totally believable.

It was beyond belief. I had no way of explaining my presence there this early in the morning. The two girls were walking their dog. They had good reason to be.

No matter. Either way, I wasn't looking forward to a lecture or a warning to stay away because...because I'd had enough of that. The repetition was starting to get annoying.

Enough of strange things that made no sense and that science couldn't explain. I was a nobody and wanted a normal life.

"Michael Jacobs, right?" Alex asked, her voice even.

I nodded and finally looked up. Her eyes were thankfully devoid of any rage—a massive relief. If anything, they were curious, studying me like I was about to sprout horns. I thought about those same hazel eyes on another girl that made me feel warm inside, how shy—

Wall, Michael! Keep up your wall. She might be reading your thoughts right now.

"I think we got off on the wrong foot this morning. I'm Alex Calloway."

That was a one-hundred-eighty turn from *go-away* to a *nice-to-meet-you*. I frowned, confused. To be honest, I kind of wished she'd leave me alone right now. However, it seemed she didn't hear that thought since her face remained blank.

She offered me her hand. No wonder they called her weird. Kids in high school didn't shake hands. Maybe they bumped fists and slapped each other's shoulders, but no one would give such a formal greeting. Well, whatever.

She might get mad if I left her hanging, so I took her hand and shook it instead.

"I know your name," I said lightly, matching her tone. "You and your sister are in my English class. Second period."

What I didn't say was that everybody knew about the two sisters. They always kept to themselves, ignoring everyone else. They didn't even talk about their lives before they came to Golden Birch. Some people even joked that they'd just spawned into Golden Birch like characters in a video game. But to me, there was something more to them than met the eye.

"So, which school did you attend before coming here?" I asked, remembering their lack of social media.

"Somewhere in the upper north," she said vaguely. She leaned forward, and I almost sprinted out of the cafeteria. But her gaze wasn't threatening. It remained riveted on the back of my hand. "Nice tattoo you got there. Your parents must be open-minded, huh?"

I automatically rubbed the mark. It suddenly felt itchy, like a recovering wound. I thought about our encounter this morning. How her eyes widened when she saw my hand running through my hair. I grew more uneasy at her sudden interest in it. But what if she knew anything about it? I glanced at her hands, clad in fingerless gloves. Nice way to hide a mark if she happened to have one, too.

"Foster parents," I said in the same vague tone she'd used on me. "They don't mind." I hoped that wasn't too much of a lie. In any case, they'd find out in ten days, and by then, I'd have a good excuse as to why there was a mark on my hand. Not that I'd had any choice in its sudden appearance. Oh, how was I going to explain this to the Jacobs? I decided that I'd cross that bridge when I got to it.

"Hey, do you think I can meet up with them?" she asked suddenly.

I froze, but despite my shock I did my best to keep my expression steady. She really *was* weird. Who asks to meet someone's parents right off the bat like that?

"Yeah, why not?" I replied, dumbfounded. "Your folks around?"

"I have a guardian like you. Clara's her name. I mean, for now. I'm sure she'd like to meet your parents."

I was stumped again. Her guardian had a name for *now*? Did she change her name often? What did that even mean?

"Sure, I guess they could meet her, too," I finally said.

"Okay, thanks for the invite." Her sweet voice sounded so...wrong. Clearly, she was forcing herself to be nice. And what kind of thanks was that? She'd basically invited herself over, dammit.

"So, who were those two men this morning? Were you guys in trouble?"

Of course, I knew they were. But if I told her I'd seen her lying unconscious on the ground, there'd be too many questions.

"Oh, you saw them. Nah, they were just random passersby."

"Huh. I like going on morning walks, too."

To be honest, I loved sleeping in and the weekends more. Well, I could wind up a good lie, too. Weren't the two sisters lucky that I happened to be 'passing by,' too? Now that I thought about it, it had nothing to do with luck. Something woke me up this morning, this premonition. As if my sixth sense knew these two girls were in trouble. I liked my 'connection' with Allegra and being her secret knight in shining armor, but being connected to Alex? Not so much.

"Mhm. The dog needed some exercise."

Yep, the dog she was talking to and had a medal in its jaw. The dog that'd nodded as she spoke.

"So, you do have a dog. I thought I saw it two days ago. In the courtyard, remember?"

Her eyebrows furrowed briefly before she was back to her smiling self. Somehow, while Allegra looked adorable when she smiled, Alex's face looked...contorted. Must be the eyes, I thought. They remained fierce and calculated and didn't fit with her gleaming white teeth.

Was it a good thing that she wasn't slapping me or prodding around in my mind? Or was it a bad thing that she was trying to be nice? I watched her lips move, just in case she sneaked a thought into my mind. I was on guard but felt no fear. I trusted my instincts.

"Bring Allegra along," I suddenly blurted out. *Really Michael? Couldn't you be more obvious? What's wrong with your mouth?* "Uh, my parents would love to meet her too."

Her smile froze. She blinked, surprised by my outburst. Couldn't blame her. I was surprised, too. *Why invite them at all? Why would she want to meet the Jacobs anyway?* "Is there something—"

Alex recovered quickly. "Sure, she'll come. Great. We'll work on that English essay together. See you this afternoon, then." With those words, she spun on her heels and disappeared.

This afternoon? I thought she meant for our parents to meet each other in a few weeks or so. I cursed inwardly. Maybe I could raincheck or something.

I lowered my head and stuffed some greasy fries into my mouth. Somehow, she'd played me and invited herself over, but I wasn't sure how.

No wonder the other students stayed away from the Calloway sisters. I wasn't too worried about her coming over this afternoon. She didn't know where I lived, and even if she did find out, I decided I'd go back to the crumbling Westview Hospital and continue practicing.

So, in conclusion, I wouldn't be home at all. And if the Calloways turned up... I wasn't about to feel guilty about it. No big deal. I'd leave a note for her on the door.

I glanced down at my empty tray, and my heart sank. Yeah, I was going to run out of food, and if I wasn't careful, I'd run out of pocket money, too.

That was my plan for this afternoon: practice and stock up on some high-energy foods. Nuts would be a good choice, and I'd always wanted to get some of those cheap, high-calorie bars. The bell rang, interrupting my thoughts. I stood up, ready to clean my tray.

Kids in orphanages are ruthless. They'll do anything to survive, including getting adopted.

The thought popped into my mind, and I stopped short. Where—What? Anything to survive? Getting adopted? Where did that sudden thought come from? I hadn't even thought about it since I was ten.

But there was only one instance I could think of. I once knew this kid, Ben. He was a year older, and I would always share meals with him—whatever was left of it anyway, once the older kids got their hands on it.

And he'd backstabbed me.

"Hey, Michael," Ben said in a chirpy voice. "Saved you some meat and mashed potatoes."

My stomach growled. All day, I sat in solitary confinement for something the bullies did and was famished. Even then, I checked the clock hung up on the wall. I was one of the few who could read the numbers and the time.

"We're going to miss the placement, Ben. And you can't either."

Ben at eight years old was a year older than me, and as you got older in the Lost Children Orphanage, your chances of getting 'placed' or adopted in a family decreased. Today was a big day and the last chance for both of us.

"Nah," Ben replied, shrugging. "Nurse says they're late. Come on, eat up." I hesitated, and he brought the plate closer. "For all the times you sneaked food for us."

I couldn't resist the enticing smell. My mouth watered, so I picked up the fork, sat on the floor, and dug in.

I was sick after eating the food. Days after Ben got a

placement, I learned he never really liked me. In fact, he'd been so jealous that he'd put something in my food. I'd really, really thought of him as a good friend. Even as a brother. The idea that he probably pretended to like me stung even more than the fact that he'd *poisoned* me in the end. I thought I was caring. Then, the Jacobs took me in months later when I was seven, and I never looked back. The silver lining, I guess.

Why think of Ben now? Was he somewhere around the school? I shook the thought from my head.

But whatever sent me to the park this morning also sent me this thought. I was certain of it. Did that mean I was a puppet? Who was in control anyway?

I sighed. You'd think having resources and money, you'd be in control of everything. But nope. One tsunami, one cyclone, could erase entire towns. Just a decade ago, before the drone scrubbers and filters, even the air had been too filthy to breathe.

As for the shield, I didn't think I had enough control. Sure, I knocked those two men down, but I still needed more practice. It seemed to have its own will.

The end of another boring school day. I stepped out of

the main entrance doors to find Alex and Allegra loitering near the school buses. *Really*? Did their guardian, Clara, with the temporary name, want to meet my parents right now? Like, *right now*?

I had no intention of going home. Still...it would've been nice to spend the afternoon with Allegra. No, *no*, *no*. With the Jacobs away, I wasn't about to have guests. Ignoring Katie's texts was hard enough work.

So, I ducked and moved away, heading toward West-view Hospital.

Practicing was a blast. As soon as I drew close to the building, the red swirls appeared. This time, I munched on a few bars and drank an entire bottle of water beforehand. Shaping the shield into a lasso, I picked up a large stone, threw it in the air, changed the lasso into a platform, and caught it.

Sure, I had a crush on Allegra, but that didn't explain why the thought of her seemed to reinvigorate me so much. Maybe coming to her rescue this morning had grown my confidence.

Two hours later, despite the cool air, beads of sweat started to form on my forehead, so I decided to call it a day. I contemplated dropping by the grocery store. On second thought, since school was ending early tomorrow for school report distribution, the groceries could wait till then. My phone pinged, and I sent a quick reply to

Janet. Everything was good. They were sipping margaritas while I was crouched down next to the budget version of the Tower of Pisa. Great.

But I wasn't envious anymore. Too many strange things had happened in the past few days. To be honest, I could use a vacation myself, but still. If I *were* on vacation, I might not have discovered my abilities. And at this point, I couldn't imagine living without them.

I stood up, stretched my aching arms, and grabbed my backpack.

That was when the sound of roaring engines reached my ears. I looked toward the road. About seven to eight military-style vehicles were driving up to the abandoned hospital. Huffing, I crouched behind the pile of debris, hoping they'd just go away quickly.

To my dismay, the large Humvees turned into the driveway and pulled into the deserted parking lot.

I was trapped.

CHAPTER 9

S oldiers in dark green camouflage with assault rifles slung across their shoulders stepped out from the vehicles. They spread out, unloaded crates, and carried them into the building. Extremely methodical. Others set up road barriers and took guard around the perimeter.

Now, this wasn't an unusual sight. When Westview collapsed, and the ground shook under Golden Birch, plenty of soldiers and scientists turned up to investigate the situation. Still, they never found a cause other than overuse of the underground water reservoirs. The scientists said it could explain why the area was so unstable.

I wanted no trouble. There'd be too many questions if I were caught in this cut-off area—questions about breaking the rules or whether I had a death wish wandering around this part of the town. But suddenly, a golden glow caught my attention, and I froze. Someone wearing a golden cloak stepped out. A bald man. The same one from this morning, the one I'd injured with my shield.

No scar marred his face, though. A twin, maybe? I wondered. He couldn't have healed so quickly, could he? The second man with the golden cloak appeared.

Whoever these people were, they had no problem attacking two teen girls in the early morning hours. Should I report them to the patrol squads? Looking at all the soldiers, though, I hesitated. They seemed to have the upper hand.

Then, something caught my attention. The man was holding a silver tube in his hand. My blood turned to ice as I recognized it. Of course, how could I have forgotten about the silver object? It blocked my ability up to a limited range, sure, but I was outmatched by far. Confronting them wasn't worth it.

Something told me there was a connection between me and these men. Just like the connection between me and Allegra. Well, um, hopefully not the *exact* same connection. I was hoping the one with Allegra was more positive. Not Alex. She was terrifying and a handful.

Stick around, or run away? Even as my mind warred with the question, my feet remained put. These men were after Allegra, and I wanted to know why. Yet, staying out of the way would be great for my survival.

I was about to move away, still in my crouched position, but then the soldiers moved past, the sound of rifles moving in sync with heavy boots.

Nope. I don't want to die.

I cursed inwardly and hoped the shadows of the debris would keep me concealed for a while. Not only was I trapped, but there were more soldiers blocking the only viable exit. More soldiers spread out around the tall walls and the building's perimeter, probably checking for intruders.

Intruders like me, of course.

So, I had no choice but to retreat inside the building. Ducking behind the low walls near the entrance, I stepped into a large, empty room that looked like a hall. The billowing, oversized curtains hanging around the windows were the only hiding place, and even then, it wasn't exactly a great one.

Why were these men here? Were they here to destroy the building? I heard somewhere that cleaning crews were always paid well these days.

The thought crossed my mind just as I realized I was *inside* the building. If they were going to destroy the building, I'd be blown to bits.

I weighed my options again. I was pretty sure neither of the men in golden cloaks had seen me this morning. Better face them and admit I was trespassing than die via demolition, right?

But I stayed back. The red swirls around my hands had grown darker since the men arrived. Plus, the grim, determined, and scarred faces jarred my nerves. These people were dressed like soldiers, but their clothes held no insignia of any sort. They certainly weren't the government soldiers who'd patrolled Golden Birch a few months ago.

A private militia, perhaps? Their steps were swift, decisive, and focused. The soldiers grouped in twos and threes performed their tasks in silence like they were on a dangerous mission.

To my dismay, instead of setting explosives around the building like I expected them to, they entered the room I was in. As if today's luck could get any worse. My stomach roiled as I watched two soldiers set up tables and chairs. Another ripped open boxes and took out coiled cables and wires.

Explosives? No, I decided. The soldier went on to hook the yards of wires to screens, laptops, and computers. The tables were arranged in neat triangles. Everything was so coordinated.

A few screens flickered, lighting up the room, and the sound of a rumbling generator echoed from the corner of the room.

A symbol on the screen drew my attention: a triangle inside a circle, and inside the triangle, a small plus sign. What the—how did they know about the symbol on the back of my hand? Then, the symbol shifted to another.

The same triangle within a circle, but inside the triangle were two small, entwined loops like an infinity sign. Then, another symbol appeared. Mesmerized, I watched the screen and counted the number of symbols. Six in total, transitioning like a glitching slideshow. I took a deep breath. It was just a coincidence, right? But there were too many coincidences already—something was at play. Someone was planning... It didn't matter. Something was up, but I didn't know what.

I should've left, but at the same time, I needed answers.

"Get the other two generators!" one woman shouted, and soldiers quickly obeyed her demands. "We need more power here."

"Are the scanners working?" a man asked in a low voice. The way he held himself with his hands behind his back told me he was in charge.

"They'll be up and running soon, sir," the woman answered, her voice clipped as if his question was an order. She blinked but couldn't hide the fear in her eyes.

Fear of him or of what was going to happen? I didn't know. The red swirls around my hand were thick and taut, ready to spring into action. I held them tight. I didn't want to draw any attention and couldn't risk more trouble.

The room emptied as the other soldiers rushed away to find their equipment.

The man turned and stared at the screen. I caught a red glint in his left eye and a blackened scar on his forehead. My gaze trailed to his prosthetic leg, which was made entirely of silver metal, stained dark red near the joints. Whether it was rust or blood—or both—I didn't want to know.

My curiosity grew. If only I could get my hands on one of the laptops—

"The men are waiting, sir," the female soldier said.

As if on cue, the man slowly walked out of the room. One by one, the soldiers filed out after him, and the vast room was empty. This was my chance. I needed to know their mission, especially if it included the mark on my hand. Crouched behind musty-smelling thick curtains, I waited for a while longer before making my move and sneaking to the computers.

The previous day, I was thinking of the irony and oxymoron that sneakers never let you sneak. Now, my own sneakers betrayed me. They squeaked with every step, making me cringe as I made my way to the tables.

Only one computer was ready to use, while the others were still booting up. I opened the documents folder. A list of sub-folders appeared under location names such as Kryphynius, Golden Birch, Cradix, and so on. Inside each were files with the name "Aequus."

I opened the Golden Birch sub-folder and read about

recent earthquakes and sinkholes like the one that collapsed Westview. Strange phenomena such as twisting tornadoes and flash floods. One file caught my attention: portals. I'd heard of strange cults and groups that believed in aliens, portals, and weirder stuff online. But a cult so heavily armed with weapons and equipped with computers and satellites? I had to report this to the patrols. Or someone.

The sound of approaching footsteps made me flinch. I scrambled to quickly close all the folders and retreat to another set of curtains closer to the exit door.

I was so focused on securing the curtains in front of me that I didn't realize at first that the door had swung open. A clopping sound echoed in the silence.

I peered through to see three men walk in: the man with the metal leg and blackened scar on his forehead, flanked by the two bald men in golden robes. Thankfully, their backs were to me, and since the lights were dim and focused on the computers, I figured I was concealed enough. I should've been afraid, but all I could feel was envy that the two bald men's boots were so silent. Seriously, I needed a pair of those. More soldiers filed in, gathering around the tables, everyone making barely a noise other than a bit of shuffling.

There was so much reverence and fear in the air. The idea that this was some kind of military cult was becoming more believable by the second.

Then, the shuffling noises stopped abruptly. Curious, I peeked around the curtain as subtly as I could. Fortunately, the soldiers' attention was on the opposite side of the room, where they'd placed a raised platform. The man with the scar climbed onto it with some effort and faced them, his chin raised and his lips set in a thin line. All the soldiers stood, back straight. This man was their leader, alright.

He raised one hand to his heart, and the two bald men flanking him did the same. Other than the hum of the computers, it was silent, the air heavy.

It was bad timing for me to sneak out, especially with my terrible, squeaky shoes.

"Today marks the dawn of a new era. Our era," the man said, his voice booming as if he held a megaphone. He raised both arms high. "Our Lord Aequus has awakened!"

But suddenly, I was taken aback. The man was holding the same medallion the dog from this morning had in its jaws. My first thought was: Was it the same medal? If so, how? And: what if it had dog slobber on it? Gross.

The man's words rattle around my brain like marbles. *Lord Aequus has awakened.* A mythical monster I vaguely recalled from doing research into ancient mythology for an English project. Howls erupted around me like the thumping of a heartbeat and its mirroring echo. The men in uniforms beat at their chests. They were all distracted. Time to make my exit. I wanted nothing to do with this c ult.

I pushed the curtains back slightly and drifted silently to the door. Eyes riveted on the stage, heart pounding, I pried it open, slid through, and made my way down the hallway, staying close to the wall.

I kept my gaze focused on the exit doors and ignored the pounding in my chest. A shuffle cut into the silence, and instinctively, I dove into the shadow of a recessed doorway. *Not again!*

Thankfully, the two men heading in my direction were too fixated on the gathering and beating their chests to spot me. Their eyes were filled with fervor and reverence. They opened the door and remained there with their backs turned to me.

No way was I waiting till the noise died down. I had to be on the move.

I inched sideways, keeping my eyes on the men in case they turned around. Unlike the kids pursuing me two days ago, these cultist men looked ruthless, not to mention unhinged. Who knew if they'd shoot a teenage boy?

If they did, I wondered whether my shield could stop their bullets. I had no intention of putting that theory into action. I slinked back into the hallway, moving one step at a time as noiselessly as I could.

Protector! I've waited for you for so long. The tiny voice startled me. I looked around. *Please don't leave. It's me, your Auracle. Set me free!*

Of course, the hallway was deserted. Yet the tiny voice, which sounded like a small girl's, echoed as if it was right next to me. In fact, it was right in my ear. But with the rumbling and howling, how could it reach me?

I remained frozen, unable to move. I couldn't leave, right? Not when somebody needed my help.

Protector, don't leave. You need me. Free me!

"Where are you?" I whispered. Darn, that made me sound like a madman.

Suddenly, a hand slammed over my mouth, and my vision tilted to the ceiling as my body was yanked back into the recessed doorway. *Ouch!*

I was about to scream when a voice hissed behind me, "Shut up, will you! I'm trying to save your skin, dammit!"

I stopped struggling and remained still. Slowly, the hand moved away from my mouth, and I turned around. The room was dark, and I could barely see the boy a few steps away from me.

He was dressed in soldier's garb and had a nasty-looking belt slung around his waist, complete with a holster and a couple of sheaths with blades' handles sticking out of them.

The boy cocked his head to the side and took a step forward. The boost of confidence I had this morning in my shield evaporated.

"Michael?" he said. "From Lost Children Orphanage?"

It hit me. I should've recognized him. Just this morning, this tiny voice reminded me of the boy who had betrayed me.

Ben stood across from me. I couldn't see his features, yet I knew for sure it was him. I felt his hesitation.

"You shouldn't be here," he said, glancing at the doorway behind me.

Yeah, no kidding, man. Saying the obvious. "Yeah. Nice to see you again, Ben."

I wanted to ask him if it was true. If he poisoned me that day. If he really hated me all along. If he'd been jealous of me and didn't care about me one bit.

But instead, I said, "You've...grown up a bit. I see you've done well for yourself." Grown up was an understatement. I could tell from the way he moved that he was lean and sinewy, even for a teen his age. He brought up his hands and stared at them. Light from a nearby window outlined the scars and dark patches that marred the skin.

"Done well," he repeated slowly.

Suddenly, he tensed, squinting at the doorway.

My vision tilted, and my body slid along the hard floor

to the dark corner of the room. What the—I swore he didn't touch me. A low gasp escaped me, but thankfully, I didn't scream.

As I struggled to get up, thuds in the hallway echoed and vibrated underneath me. I froze.

"Soldier! Have you checked the perimeter?"

"Yes, ma'am. There's no one in this building." A silence ensued.

Curious, I shifted and saw Ben facing a woman in her thirties. He had his hands behind his back. The woman was accompanied by a group of soldiers.

"You say you checked, yet I have a report of an intruder from a sense sham."

Sense sham? Was this building equipped with sensors? Maybe the generator powered them? Ben's hands moved slowly as if giving me a message. I took it as my cue to leave. But how? The woman and her goons blocked the entrance.

"Step aside, soldier," the woman ordered.

To my surprise, Ben stayed put.

Even more surprising, the woman smiled, but not in a nice way. "You know what Rimes does to traitors." Ben's shoulders tensed, but he remained still, blocking the door. The woman lifted a hand, and a crackle sounded. Tiny bolts like miniature lightning played in her palm.

Run, Michael, run! But as if mesmerized, I couldn't

take my eyes off the tiny sparks flying from the woman's hand.

Every fiber of my being told me that what I was seeing was real. A world where people yielded powers.

Ben's fists clenched behind his back as if bracing himself. A shiver ran down my spine. The woman's eyes gleamed with the thrill of the challenge.

Another shiver ran down my spine. I stood close to a partially-framed fireplace, and a cold breeze wafted around me.

I rounded the frame and saw the outline of a low, crumbling wall. An exit! Ben must've known about it when he pushed me down the corner. I hesitated only for a fraction of a second, waiting for the child's voice to sound again.

When I heard nothing, I slid through, my backpack almost catching against the rough sides, and darted across the backyard. I reached the far end of the parking lot near the edge of the property before I slowed my pace and caught my breath. I still needed to get past the lone soldier patrolling the area near the barricade next to the road.

I stayed close to the trees. From my position, I saw a glow emanating from the sinkhole. The memory of two red eyes came forth in my mind, and another shiver coursed through me like ice in my veins. Maybe they were...glow sticks? Okay, probably not, but still.

It was easy to sneak past the guard near the road once he got distracted by several trucks turning into the driveway. It looked like these soldiers were here to stay.

My thoughts raced as I made my way home. As I moved away from Westview, the waves around my hands thankfully grew fainter. I was safe. For now.

The Aequus was a mythical monster. In legends, the heroes would fight these monsters with their powers. Whatever this weird cult had supposedly awakened was clearly not good.

Then I thought of my shield. If that was real, why couldn't monsters from legends also be real? Then, there were all these disasters overwhelming the cities. And portals...my mind was officially blown. In fact, I could feel an oncoming headache.

With great power comes great responsibility. And great pain and monsters, too.

Just the day before, I had enjoyed testing my powers. Heck, I even had fun seeing the fear in Jack's eyes. But since I'd woken up this morning, everything went berserk. I'd refused to think about everything that went on until now because, frankly, I was scared, and nothing made sense.

Two bald men threatening Allegra while Alex was unconscious and carrying a medallion. The same men who were now affiliated with a dangerous militia-cult group that had taken over the crumbling Westview Hospital.

A dog that nodded and seemed to understand Alex.

Alex, who spoke in my mind, then invited herself over to my house.

A sense of premonition that reminded me of Ben, whom I then met only a few hours later.

Ben, who didn't touch me, yet tossed me like a leaf across a room.

The woman with sparks crackling around her hands.

That voice, likely telepathic, that pleaded for my help and...

The list was endless. I was halfway to the city center when my headache became a hammer pounding in my head. My head exploded with pain. My hands reached for a wall, and I stood there, hoping the pain would pass.

But it didn't. The pain spread to my face and the back of my neck. It was so intense that I staggered, and before I realized it, I was on my knees, clutching my temples. *Stop! Stop!* I'd never felt such pain before. Heck, I'd never fallen ill, had a fever, or a major injury. I'd always thought I had a great immune system.

Nothing had prepared me for such blinding, excruciating pain.

A hissing sound echoed, and my vision clouded. That sound was in my head. It had an echoing quality, just like the child's voice that pleaded for my help earlier.

White spots appeared in my vision. The fog cleared, and an image of a mole flashed before my eyes. Not the burrowing animal, but a mole with a wisp of a lone hair sticking out on a man's face. Eww. Gross. I couldn't see his entire face, but the person with the mole was taking deep breaths. Angry, frustrated, murderous, in fact.

I felt the waves slither around my hands, growing strong and ready. I knew instinctively this was no ordinary man. As quickly as the image appeared in my vision, it disappeared, and I was back in a lonely alleyway in the town center.

I glanced around, but I was alone. I gathered my backpack and rushed straight back home, heart pounding.

Unlike the previous night, when I went straight to bed after a quick wash, I forced myself to have a quick bite this time. Despite my exhaustion, I checked all the doors and windows and peeked through the curtains. No one was watching the house, yet I couldn't get rid of that sense of dread.

I knew I was out of action for the night. My body was so drained that I could barely move. The worst part was that the waves around my hands remained, weaving their dance from my elbows to the tip of my fingers. Waiting. Warning.

Logic took over after a few moments. Maybe I was in danger, or somebody else was. There was no telling whether the danger was close or when the enemy would strike.

But I was of no use, exhausted as I was. I needed to recharge and refuel. It had always annoyed me, knowing humans had to sleep a third of their lives away.

I sighed, lay in bed, closed my eyes, and let the darkness swallow me.

CHAPTER 10

Several light years away, in a galaxy that was most certainly not the Milky Way, on a planet as bleak as a desert, something stirred deep underground. The movement was almost imperceptible, and one would have most likely overlooked the colorless, formless energy that wavered in the air.

Above ground, however, another meaningless battle raged over this *something*.

This Being was ancient, older than several galaxies and worlds put together. It had existed since the beginning of time. It had seen the Universe crash into being, and it had seen the Multiverse create its galaxies.

The Being, trapped in another dimension, slowly slithered into the physical world, and its first inklings of consciousness emerged. At first, it sensed a pinpoint of light, and then muffled sounds echoed somewhere in the distance. The Being inhaled slowly with its new lungs. A heart started to beat in the center of its form, rushing newly-formed blood through its veins. Bones formed, followed by organs and muscles. Limbs grew. The Being stretched taller, leathery skin streaming over its chest, arms, and legs, a wicked row of spikes flanked by two horns sprouting from its skull.

For a moment, it remained frozen, perusing its memories of the past and listening to the sounds of clashes above. The ancient Being remembered the last battle it had fought and when it had been defeated. It filtered its memories and recalled the Mages and Children who imprisoned it here. Since then, it had been sent into hibernation, living on the brink of death, buried deep in this empty planet, the Overworld, at the center of the Fireworks Galaxy.

The Mages and Children sought to prevent the Being from conquering the Multiverse. They never understood what power meant.

The Being realized that a few of the same Mages who'd imprisoned it had freed it from the breadth of eternity and its everlasting sleep. The battle between the Mages raged on above.

The ones who helped free it believed they had gained control over the Being. The latter sensed their greed and pride and grinned inwardly. How puny their minds were. How malleable. But the deed was done, and it was awake n ow.

It stirred again, its telepathic radar searching for the reincarnation of one of the Children who imprisoned it.

Zero.

This Child was the only one it considered worthy enough to fight. It wondered for a moment why the Child hadn't annihilated it and instead imprisoned it in an ever-lasting sleep, devoid of consciousness. Perhaps the Being couldn't be killed by inferior creatures. Perhaps it was too powerful for the Children. The thought sent renewed energy coursing through its veins.

It listened as the Mages battled, some claiming to fulfill a prophecy of the Being's return. It listened to and understood their speech.

The sounds of battle stopped abruptly. An unsettling silence followed. Who won? The Mages who helped its release or those who wanted it to remain in this for-saken sleep? It didn't matter to the Being. Because only the Children could stand in its path. These Mages were nothing but pathetic. At the thought, it sensed its power surging.

Suddenly, it stilled. There! On a sphere, the telepathic radar singled out a single living organism.

It had found the Child! But what species was it? Curious, the Being dug further, straining to keep its focus despite its weakened state. Its radar caught on to the vibrations of the Child once more. It sensed immense power and determination.

The Protector had always had a sickening, fierce urge to save others, even at its own expense. They would stand in its way and fight it with all their might.

At first, a surge of elation flooded the Being. It delighted in the challenge the Child presented. Soon, it would have its revenge for its imprisonment.

But...something was different. Could it be the Child had manifested itself into this weak life form known as...Homo sapiens? The Being studied the human form with its bare skin, blunt teeth, and dire musculature.

Argh. This was no challenge. That Child was in its infant state. The immense power the Being sensed was merely a fraction of what it could be. The Being watched the meek face of the young Homo sapiens Child and was suddenly on alert, its spikes straightening and its tail swinging wildly.

The Being couldn't tell why it felt threatened so suddenly. So, it made its decision. This Child couldn't be allowed to grow into power. The Being would seek out this species and destroy all of them. Then, it would take over the planet where the Children resided before conquering the Multiverse and its galaxies.

A voice boomed from above. The voice of a Mage. "Victory is upon us! It has awakened! The Aequus is now ours to take!"

The Being grinned again, showing off what remained of its teeth—now fully developed, appearing as sharp, serrated fangs. It recognized one of its many former names. Out of all of them, it liked this name the most.

Aequus, the great monster. How befitting.

Its eyes opened. The world slowly formed around it, and it recognized the roots nearby. So, the Mages and Children imprisoned it under the Endless Tree. In a corner, dangling from a root, was an orb, a gift from the stupid Mages. An orb that the Being sensed was filled with energy.

It reached its claws out, plucked the orb, and swallowed it whole. Immediately, renewed life flooded inside its newly formed body, deepening its energy reservoir and strengthening it. It had never felt so alive. The orb, most likely construed from the death of a powerful Mage, was so potent that it awakened every fiber inside the Being.

It needed more energy and more Mages. After all, it was a long way to travel to reach the Child unless...unless it could access the path through portals.

The Aequus studied the Child, tossing and turning on their bed as if in a nightmare. Only the weak succumbed to pathetic nightmares.

Sleep well, Child. I'll be coming for you soon. Rest and become strong so we shall meet as equals when the time comes.

The Child stopped tossing and turning. Their crumpled face relaxed, and their breaths became deep and peaceful. Slowly, the Aequus stretched. Perhaps the Mages who were celebrating its awakening would taste good as well.

CHAPTER 11

Day 4

I woke up refreshed. That was an understatement. My eyes flipped wide open, and I greeted the day with a big stretch. Darn, I'd never felt so good. My head was clear as a blue sky.

Tingling in my toes and fingers? All gone.

Alex shouting in my mind? I must have imagined all of it.

A dog holding a medallion in its jaw? Nothing wrong with that.

Men with bald, tattooed heads threatening two teen girls? Nothing strange about that. Worse stuff happened in the town center and parks. Thankfully, I was there. Now that I thought about it, I should really warn the girls about walking the dog early in the morning. Maybe they should both carry something to protect them.

And the cult group I saw last night? Nothing to be concerned about. With so many disasters, groups like those grew rampant, feeding on people's fear and poverty. What was concerning was that they were armed. But that was a problem for the patrols and bots, not me.

I sprang out of bed. I couldn't remember the last time I felt so refreshed. I loved days like these, and there was no way I'd miss school. It was a half-day, anyway. Plenty of time to hang out at the mall and do some grocery shopping.

After a quick wash, I sent a few quick messages to Janet and Mark. I noticed their messages' frequency had decreased, which was a good thing. I'd see them by the end of next week. I wanted to earn their trust; show them I was responsible enough to take care of myself. Well, they wouldn't have left me at home if they didn't think I could—knowing Janet, she'd be elated if I brought friends over.

That made me think of Alex and her plan to visit. I could only hope she wasn't too mad. I had no intention of having her over, of inviting anyone over to my house—except for Allegra, maybe.

While cleaning up, I put groceries at the top of my priority list. Janet left extra cash with the babysitter—what an ugly word. I wasn't a baby. Ugh. Contacting Katie would be my last resort.

The morning went without incident. No dog, no one in soldier garb, no weird bald men. In English class, I felt Alex's gaze on me, but I kept my eyes lowered. When class ended, I was the first one out. Finally, the second period was over. I ditched the bus and headed into town. I was ready to stock up on food.

Well, that was what I *meant* to do. Give a four-teen-year-old a fifty-dollar bill, and the temptation was right up there. Yep, my feet carried me to the Golden Birch Mall.

More specifically, the Breakfast Waffle House.

Someone had removed parts of the letters and vowels so that it read 'BRAKFIST WALL HOSE.' A handyman stood on a ladder, fixing the sign.

Like a moth drawn to light, I drew closer, inhaling the sweet, delicious smell of waffles and pancakes wafting from the open door. It wasn't noon yet, and breakfast foods were just what I needed. Couldn't hurt to get some food beforehand, right? Today was a good day, and this could only make it better.

As I weaved past the ladder that was partly blocking the entrance, the handyman missed a step. Unfortunately, in his stumble, he pulled the ladder sideways. The ladder wobbled. The handyman stretched out his arm in an effort to stabilize the ladder but to no avail.

I was in no danger of being hit. Still, I calculated that the probability of the ladder pitching sideways and dropping to the ground was high.

As if acting of their own will, my wrists flicked automatically, the rubber band lashing out and steadying the ladder. The shield retracted into my hands just as fast. It was all done in a fraction of a second.

I sighed in relief, watching the handyman shake his head, grip the now-steady ladder, and resume his climb down. Next, my gaze swept around the mall quickly in case someone noticed the red flash, but everyone went about their business as usual.

That was new, I supposed. My shield revealed itself not because of danger around me but to save someone. A good deed in my day, I told myself, smiling. I gave myself a mental pat on the back.

This shield was meant to protect not only me but others, too. I was meant to protect people. *Protector*, the child's voice called me. *Save me.* Had I dreamt all of it? I shook the thought out of my head.

Next, I searched for security cameras. My hood concealed my face enough, and I wondered what the feed would show. I doubt it would pick up on my red shield. Perhaps it would show the ladder wobble and then steady all by itself, but that could easily be attributed to the handyman shifting his weight or something.

Still, I couldn't shake the quiet unease worming into my gut. I should be careful when and where I used my shield. I certainly didn't want my ability to be out in the open. From the old movies Janet had played every Friday—all of my favorite superheroes—I'd seen enough to know that powers could backfire any moment you used them in public.

Then, there were government agents with dark sunglasses and shady outfits who'd kidnap and send me to labs to be experimented upon.

And let's not forget the interrogation. *How did you get your powers? Were you placed in a machine and mutated to become immortal, or were you struck by lightning? Did you happen to get a super serum or a glowing green ring? Were you bitten by a weird insect? Were you a passenger on that train that crashed two months ago? Were you the sole survivor? Were you hit by a piece of a satellite infused with dark matter?* And so on. I barely knew how I got my powers, anyway.

What really bothered me was that in all the superhero movies, there was a counterbalance. There was always a reason why the superhero acquired their powers in the first place. Images of a recent nightmare of red eyes, shrieks, and battlegrounds crossed my mind. I quickly shook my head.

Stay focused. Keep your shield a secret. While living on the streets, I learned this: if you know something nobody else does, you better keep it to yourself.

I shook my head again, and suddenly the world around me spun. I staggered and recovered my balance.

Fortunately, a teen wearing a hoodie and missing a step was a common sight. Heck, tall teens like me were supposed to be clumsy, anyway.

I sighed. Using my power seemed to affect my body's fuel reserves. My focus scattered like bugs, and my head began pounding.

Time to ingest more fuel. I walked into the shop and ordered chocolate chip waffles. Toppings were unlimited—the sole reason the Waffle House was my favorite place. I ignored the cashier's concerned stare as I covered every inch of the waffles with two kinds of syrup, more chocolate chips, sugar sprinkles, three scoops of vanilla ice cream, banana slices, crushed waffle cones, and a large strawberry milkshake to wash it all down with.

Voila! After saving the handyman, I felt I deserved a treat. Tempted as I was to gobble it all up, I savored each bite, slowly chewing and swallowing.

But I had vowed to be responsible, so in the grocery store, I grabbed a few easy microwavable meals (Janet would cringe at the nutrition facts), healthy nuts and seeds, and high-calorie bars before heading into the parking lot of the mall. The insanely sugary brunch had left me in a euphoric, almost hysterical state. I was practically skipping over the concrete.

The bright sun shone down on me, and I shielded my eyes from the blinding light. After the storm two days ago, the weather seemed to have improved. Fascinated, I watched the pavement waver before me. Wait... We were in late winter, and it wasn't hot, so that meant—

Like a wisp of smoke, a slight red wave was weaving around my hands. I dropped them to my sides.

I felt no tingle, warmth, or ache. The telltale sign that something was stirring was the cold shiver on my neck. Like someone just applied an ice cube on my skin.

Next, an image of the Mole-Man flashed in my mind, sharper this time. Last night, I only saw the wisp of hair sticking out of the mole (I know, so gross).

This time, I saw his entire face in my mind like a movie scene. He was taking deep breaths again. Why was I watching him sniffing? It was darn creepy.

But I trusted this vision, this sensation of dread. My heart skipped a beat. Mole-Man was sniffing for a good reason, and somehow, that involved me.

Then, like a camera shifting, I saw where he stood: next to the handyman on the ladder!

This moment was now. Mole-Man was inside Golden Birch Mall and very, very close by.

Instinctively, I ducked between two cars in the parking lot, my bags crinkling to my sides. Was I really seeing something happening now without even being there? Heck, it could've been this morning, or maybe the handyman had been at work two days ago—but everything told me I was in danger.

As if to confirm my suspicions, the sound of boots stomping on the ground echoed in the deserted parking lot. Muffled voices of two men followed. Both seemed to be arguing.

Crouched next to a car's wheels, I shifted and risked a glance.

Mole-Man was on the other side of the car, far too close to me. I saw him clearly now. Sideburns that ran down his jawline, a thin goatee down his chin, and thick, black-rimmed glasses. Again and again, he took deep, slow breaths, head facing the sky, inhaling through his nose and exhaling through his mouth. His actions reminded me of a human bloodhound. Or that of a werewolf.

Suddenly, Mole-Man whipped his head from side to side. His inhale lasted over five seconds. His head slowly turned in my direction, and I ducked behind the car again. The waffles must've made me unfocused. Mole-Man was obviously some sort of tracker, and he was after me, following my scent. And given the current situation, he'd almost certainly sniffed me out.

CHAPTER 12

T he thought made me wince. I should be wearing more deodorant, more cologne, more everything (especially aftershave lotion that I or any fourteen-year-old didn't own) from now on to hide my scent. Just in case.

What flustered me more was that I didn't think he wasn't real when I had a vision of him the previous night. I'd thought it was someone I'd passed by and forgotten or someone famous from a movie. Now, seeing him for real convinced me that I'd never seen him before in my life.

My shield, this red, wispy smoke around my hands, was a warning. This man was up to no good, a dangerous man for sure. Worse, he was also after me.

"Can't see him, man. You say he's close by?" the other one asked. He had a trailing nasal accent.

"Sure, I can smell his sweat," Mole-Man growled, "and his soap. I tell ya, he's around."

Cringing at the crinkling of my bags and still crouch-

AJ DASHER & KRIS RUHLER

ing low, I moved to the next parked car. I continued falling back by moving parallel to the vehicles as quickly and soundlessly as possible until the men were out of sight.

Cries of frustration reached my ears. "I tell ya, he's there. Upwind of me."

Mole-Man was right. The wind was blowing toward him—and carrying my scent along. Which probably meant he was locked in on me, and I was trapped.

I fought a growing sense of despair as I looked around for something to defend myself and saw nothing. Other than my shield, which was unpredictable, I had no weapon.

Think fast, Michael. Then I remembered the day before in Broadway Park with the two bald men. I'd been powerless until I moved away. Maybe it worked the same way. Mole-Man's tracking ability must have a limited range.

If not, I was done for.

Instead of the hero in a movie, I'd be the pathetic human prey in a zombie movie—the idiot character who dies from their own sheer stupidity, the one who'd stop and rest while the zombies can move and hunt all night and all day.

Grocery shoppers poured into the parking lot. The rumble of trolleys and the crinkling of bags sounded. A baby's scream cut through the area. Surely, more people in the parking lot would mask my scent, right?

My luck turned when the breeze became a swirling gust. The cars started moving, puffing out fumes. I peeked at Mole-Man and was relieved to see him distracted and squinting in the opposite direction.

It was now or never. Keeping low and clutching my bags close to my sides (on second thought, I'd decided to keep them despite the noise they made), I headed for the main road and darted away.

My thoughts scrambled, and for a moment, I had no clue where to go.

Who were these men? How'd they pick up my scent? Why? Was I being paranoid? Were they really after me?

Yes, they are, moron. You're in deep trouble. They probably somehow found out you were snooping around at Westview yesterday and sent people after you.

Realizing I was wandering aimlessly, I backtracked. My legs were shaking. Despite the sun's warmth, my jaw and shoulders started shaking, too. I needed to get somewhere safe. And that was home.

I veered into my home street and was relieved to find no strangers lurking around. Still, I waited for a quarter hour, watching and waiting.

Even before I opened the door, a strange sensation overwhelmed me. After a moment of fatigue, I finally stepped inside the house, determined to scrub everything clean: clothes, body, hair, and everything in between to get rid of my scent. Putting all the groceries away helped to calm my nerves. I decided to stuff all the snacks in my backpack—I'd never know when I'd be in danger if I was low on energy, like at the Breakfast Waffle House—and headed to my room.

Perhaps it was my enhanced senses, but I kept picking up a strange smell. Like my nose knew something was wrong.

Damn, I truly hoped I didn't have a sniffing-tracking ability too. I found it kind of gross. I mean, going around sniffing a bunch of (probably unpleasant) smells? No thanks, I'm good. That didn't do well for anyone's image.

I took a wary step inside my room. The strange, musky smell wafting around was faint. Horror filled me as I recognized that musky scent.

I now understood what Mole-Man meant by 'soap.'

He'd been in my room. He'd been in my bathroom.

A knot formed in my throat as I rummaged around, searching for anything odd, and I found it in the corner of my room.

Call me a weirdo, but I liked folding my dirty laundry before putting it into the basket. That way, I could stuff in more clothes. My logic was that I'd need only one load in the washing machine if the clothes were neatly folded.

Right now, I was staring at a laundry basket that was in disarray. A shiver of disgust ran through me, and I swallowed hard.

Mole-Man had been through my laundry. Gross *and* creepy.

A bunch of thoughts swirled around my mind. *Think, Michael.* First, my house wasn't safe anymore. Did they place any cameras or bugs around? The two men knew where I lived. But they tracked me to the mall instead of just staking out my house. So, they were clearly rushed for time.

Second, I needed to pack my bags and get out of here. But what about Janet and Mark? Would they be safe when they returned? I decided that this problem could be tackled later. In movies, loved ones were used as leverage, tortured and—

Stop! Hands trembling, I took out my phone and read Janet's messages. The one from the previous night mentioned something about extending their holiday. I quickly sent a long, happy text about how amazing that was and reassured them that I was doing okay. Lots of exclamation marks, memes, and dancing pandas to show how happy I was with the news. I was anything but. Maybe relieved that they were safely away until I figured out...something.

Time to move. I was a sitting duck. I grabbed a

couple of clean T-shirts, pants, toiletries, and dashed downstairs. My school backpack was overflowing with snacks, so I grabbed a camping one that belonged to Mark and neatly packed everything, including a refillable water bottle. I had no clue how long I'd be on the road or where I'd be going, and water was always a must.

Water... It was like I was back to living on the streets and planning my necessities. It struck me then that, most likely, I would be. I looked around the house that I might never come back to. Not a house, but a home that had sheltered me for the past seven years and one in which I'd felt comforted and loved.

A painful lump formed in my front, and I fought back the stinging in my eyes. Why me? I was a nobody. I never wanted any trouble. But now I was being hunted by a sniffing Mole-Man, and my life would never be the same.

Get a grip. It's just a house you're leaving behind. You'll always have good memories. And it's not like this is goodbye forever, right?

Luck had a strange way of twisting your life. I'd been lucky to find good foster parents. I thought of Ben, of whom I'd been so envious. He'd looked so scared the previous night.

A tangy, acrid smell tickled my nose, interrupting my thoughts and making me panic. I didn't remember leaving anything on. I rushed downstairs and burst into the kitchen. There was no fire, but the microwave had burnt pizza splatters on the plate. The missing pizza in my freezer confirmed my suspicion.

Not only did they break into my home, but they burnt my pizza snacks. Just who did they think they were? Who were these people who dared to break into my house and burn my pizza snacks?

This made my blood boil. I was fuming as I returned to packing my bag. Let them come back, and I'd bash them all. I was almost tempted to set up a series of elaborate and painful traps around the house if they ever came back here. It'd be a well-deserved punishment.

After a few moments, my fury faded, and as I shouldered my bag, I peeked out the window to check if the streets were clear. I left a note for Katie, then thought about school. Ah, my report card was being handed out tomorrow.

Then I shook my head. I had to face reality. School didn't matter anymore—if Janet or Mark sent a text asking about my grades, I'd resort to lying. Being hunted by two grown men with tracking abilities took top priority, way above a school report card. Being on the run was better than facing these men.

It was early afternoon, and as I set off, I thought of the relatively safe places where I could stay for the night. Broadway Park was at the top of the list, but the night patrol bots were sure to kick me out. Then there was Westview. I could always sneak in and lay low, away from the soldiers. But what if they sniffed me out? As much as I tried, I couldn't get the voice that cried for my help out of my head.

A void opened inside of me. I hated that hollow feeling, that emptiness that threatened to swallow me whole.

It wasn't as if I had any choice, right?

With a heavy heart, I slapped on as much body spray as possible, even rubbing it into my skin. I didn't know when I'd return, so I wrapped a thin coat around my waist and stuffed my hat and gloves in the pockets. Then, backpack secured, I locked the door behind me and headed out.

CHAPTER 13

T he sun was facing me as I headed west. Poor excuse for not seeing the two figures that appeared out of the blue in front of me.

"Michael Jacobs?" one of them asked.

I shielded my eyes, squinting. All I could see were their blurred faces and black leather jackets. Flashes of red thwarted my sight.

My heart skipped a beat as I realized two things. First, the road was wavering before me as if heat radiated from it—the angry waves emanated from my hands, which were held up to my forehead. Second, the sickening smell of sweat that wafted toward me was the same one I'd picked up earlier.

Darn, I was slow today. Even a sloth could beat me. My instincts told me to run, and I took an involuntary step back. Then, I steeled myself. Hard to hide from someone who could track your scent, so I might as well face them. I also needed explanations. I needed to confront the people who violated my privacy. So, I braced myself in a fighting stance instead of running, hoping to put the few taekwondo lessons Janet had encouraged me to take to good use. I had before, when I was facing Jack. But now, I wished I'd been more diligent and earned all my belts.

"What do you want with me?" I asked, glad to hear my voice was steady despite the tendrils of fear shooting inside me. "Why are you following me?"

You don't argue with guys who broke into your house. I swallowed. Why was I chatting again instead of running?

"Ah, so you *were* in the mall. We are, let's say, 're-cruiters,'" Mole-Man said, making air quotes with his index fingers next to his ears, "for a...secret group. Our boss, Commander Rimes, wants to see you. So, come with us. He just wants to have a...chat."

He dragged out the last word, and his sneering tone told me it would be more than just a chat. Huh... Rimes? Where had I heard that name before? Ah, yes, from the woman confronting Ben. She looked so gleeful at using her sparks to inflict fear.

But this Commander Rimes sounded much worse. Could he have been the man with the scar and metal leg? Standing up on that stage, he'd had the air of a leader as everyone else chanted below him.

I glanced at the other man. He was so tall that I had to crane my neck to look at his face. All edges and angles, with a sharp jaw, elongated neck, and long chin. Dark blue eyes bore down on me, eyebrows furrowed as if in concentration. Maybe he was trying to read my mind, or maybe he was just constipated.

"And if I don't?" I asked.

"Then let's say Commander Rimes will be very upset. And we don't want him upset, do we? He doesn't make requests, and this wasn't one. You have an incredible gift, something our group has been searching for."

"What gift? I'm just an ordinary boy."

"Tsk, tsk. With waves like those on your hands?" Dammit, he could see them.

There goes your cover, moron.

"Uh…" *Keep them talking.* "How do I know this group is legit?"

"Come with us and you'll find out."

My heart sank. *Well, I guess it was a good life.*

He grinned. His mocking tone grated on my nerves. His attempts at making polite conversation had failed miserably. I'd always had this knack of knowing when someone was genuine or fake. These two were making my talent seem like child's play with their blatantly obvious lies.

Leaves rustled, and footsteps thudded against the ground behind me. I sensed another two people there. I was cornered.

They're bounty hunters. Run!

The thought flashed through my mind. But run where, and for how long?

Even if I did run, these two would catch up to me no matter how fast I was or how well I knew Golden Birch. They had my scent, and that was enough.

Nope. I was better off fighting them and then running far, far away from this town. My shield would protect me, right? So, I held out my hands in front of me, my fingertips shimmering red. That was the plan: take the two in front of me down and make a run for it before the other two could reach me. A surprise attack would work in my favor.

I thinned my shield into a lasso and swung it. It wrapped around Mole-Man, and his body slammed into the pole closest to me. A satisfying crunch followed.

Awed at the shield's strength, I retracted the lasso and swung it toward the tall guy. But while Mole-Man was slow, this one was lean, muscular, and fast. He evaded my strike with ease.

He retrieved a strange gun from his jacket—silver with a closed end. A dart poked out from it. At least they wanted me to meet this Commander Rimes in one piece and not dismembered.

I flung the lasso at him a second time, but he side-stepped again. I drew the shield as a blanket and hurled it at him. He lurched aside just in time, but the corner of my shield slammed into his shoulder, making him stumble. Tall Man straightened, eyes darkened, and continued prepping his dart-gun.

I drew the shield around my body. Behind me, footsteps thundered against the ground, closer now. Were there more recruiters, or were they bystanders? No time to play defense. I shrugged my backpack off and tossed it to the ground. It would weigh me down in a chase.

Suddenly, my attacker swore out loud and dropped his gun. My jaw dropped, and I ducked in time as a pulsing, blue plasma blast swooped above my head. Instinctively, I crouched onto the ground and swept my leg out.

Mole-Man stumbled against the pole, his hands flailing and his body leaning dangerously to the side. Before he regained his balance, blue forks of electricity slammed into him. He flew backward at least ten feet and landed on his back. He didn't get up. I turned around and raised both hands, my shield wrapped around me like a blanket.

My mouth opened slightly to say something, but I froze. My shield began to fade as I caught sight of a girl with hazel eyes.

For a split second, I thought it was Alex.

It was Allegra.

Blue bolts of electricity sparked from her fingers. Her hazel eyes were fierce and her wavy, dark hair was flickering a flaming blue. I was awestruck yet again.

"Hi, Michael," Allegra chirped, and the blue disappeared from her hair. She was smiling, all her rage suddenly gone. But the blue shoots of electricity spurting from the tips of her fingers were still there, and she acted like it was normal. "We came by your house yesterday and waited, but you weren't home."

I didn't reply. I couldn't take my eyes off the sparks. "Uh, I—"

"Pick up your bag," Alex said to me in an even tone, appearing behind Allegra and glaring at me. "More Trackers are heading this way."

Alex...then it hit me. The voice that had shouted at me to run. It had to have been Alex's! So, it hadn't been my imagination after all. I wasn't sure if that was reassuring or not.

I picked up my bag, flustered and unable to speak. But, like a broken record, the thought swirled in my mind: *I could hear Alex's voice in my head. Again.*

I wasn't imagining things. So, that happened yesterday morning when she'd screamed in my head. It suddenly felt like an invasion.

Get a grip, Michael. Focus. These two just saved your ass.

I went over that thought. Yep, that thought was mine, not hers.

Wait, Trackers? Bounty hunters? "How did you find

me?" I asked.

"I followed the Tracker, duh," Alex said. "Ivanov's a good Tracker, I'll admit. I even found others with abilities just by following him. Well, he's a good Tracker, but also an idiot. His mind was weak enough for me to realize he was tracking you."

I hauled my bag over my shoulder and studied the road ahead. "I don't understand. What do they want from me?" A near-hysterical laugh bubbled up from my throat, and I wasn't sure why. Maybe it was from the shock. "This can't be real."

"You tell me, Michael Jacobs," Alex retorted back. "You've got this shield stuff, and you flung that guy against a pole effortlessly." She motioned to Mole-Man's unconscious body. "Does that look unreal to you? We need to move. Like, now. That's what you need to understand."

I glanced at Tall-Man, lying still on the ground. "Is he dead? You know, like electrocuted?"

"Of course not!" Allegra said, sounding offended. She made a hesitant pout. "I only zapped him a little bit."

A little bit, huh? The guy flew ten feet away. And she was...pouting. Funny.

"You couldn't have beaten him," Alex said, following my gaze. "So don't feel bad. He's a Precog. He can anticipate every single one of your moves and every punch you can think of. He knows it's coming and dodges it. This one's mean, trained assassin and a bounty hunter, too. Didn't I tell you to run?"

Yes, she did. As I remembered her words, I noted that her voice in my head had an echoing quality, like a static sound. I was about to protest about her ordering me around when Tall-Man stirred and struggled to get up. Mole-Man grunted, clawing at the pavement and pushing himself up.

"How do I know I can trust you two?" I said quickly, uncertain but aware that Tall-Man was recovering quickly. "I don't even know you. There's a guy ready to shoot me with a dart gun, and all these people keep following me, including you two. I'm going nowhere until I get answers."

The waves around my hands alerted me of the imminent danger quickly recovering, but I figured that'd motivate them to answer. I crossed my arms and glared at the two sisters. They exchanged worried glances.

Alex suddenly stilled. Then she looked around and sighed. "You want to do this in the middle of the street? C'mon. People are starting to stare. Oh, hey, I see someone getting their phone out. They might be calling the patrol bots. Why don't we go find somewhere to hide?"

"Broadway Park's this way," I said. "At this time of the day, it should be quiet." But Mole-Man had my scent.

Would I be safe in the park? Would either of them be safe around me? My thoughts trailed to Allegra.

Alex took out a cylindrical tube, and a hiss sounded, accompanied by misty puffs of strong-smelling smoke.

"Hey!" I protested, ducking away. Chloroform? Poison? You never knew what somebody might do to you when you weren't looking. Was she going to kill me because I thought of Allegra?

Alex rolled her eyes. "Relax! Really? You thought I'd *poison* you? It's just hairspray to mask your scent." She started briskly walking away, and I lined up after her. After sticking her tongue out at the two men, Allegra followed behind me.

"How—I—you read my mind." It was more of a statement than a question, really. We'd only turned a couple corners, but darn, these girls moved fast. At least I was used to quick movement. But for some reason, I was matching their pace and not the other way around.

"Yes, I did. But you thought of my sis. And I picked up on it. Again!"

Allegra smiled, her eyes bright and teeth shining white. "You were?"

My heart skipped a beat. I forced myself to turn back to Alex. "So, you spoke to me in my mind...telling me about the bounty hunters and to run... I mean, thanks for the warning, but it's just not right. Just..."

"I don't like it any more than you do," Alex snapped. "I only do it when necessary. I push thoughts into people's minds, yes, but rarely read their minds. I only did it now because you thought of Flame."

"Flame? Who's Flame?"

"My sister. She's going by Allegra for now."

"For now...? Ah, just stop getting into my head! Even if I think about Allegra...Flame—whatever! Understood? It's not right!"

Alex sent me a quizzical look. "Alright, then. Like I said, it's not something I like to do. It's like taking a bath with someone else in a bathtub." She shuddered, her face twisting in disgust. She looked genuine enough.

"Why did you rescue me?" I asked, changing the subject.

"You have the mark," she said in a matter-of-fact tone. Like that made any sense. "You're one of us. Lead the way to the park." She paused and gave me a once-over. "You look like you're about to faint. On second thought, maybe I should take you to our home. It's on Islington Avenue, much closer than the park. You okay?"

I wanted to protest. I had no intention of going to their place and meeting Clara, their guardian. But my mouth felt sticky, and my head a tad bit light. I recognized the signs of being low on fuel. I reached for my backpack but had little energy to unzip it.

Still in shock, I felt Allegra take my arm, her eyes filled with concern. She pulled me down the road and somewhere away from the park. I didn't try to escape. My body felt heavy, and an ache I'd never felt before ran down my arms and legs.

Too weary to focus or protest, I let them lead me down the road, barely hanging onto consciousness. I'd hate it if I were to pass out and these two girls had to carry me the whole way.

My shield was gone, but I knew I had to remain on my guard. I'd find out soon enough whether these two were friends or foes.

CHAPTER 14

My brain was so foggy that I barely registered the directions. I only knew that the location was east of the town. All I needed was to eat something. Yet, while the girls led me to their place, I stayed quiet for two reasons. One, I enjoyed having Allegra's—no, Flame's arm around mine. Being close to her sent a warm, fuzzy feeling coursing through me.

Then there was Alex frowning at me. I could see the gears turning in her head. I was sure she was thinking something along the following lines: *what a weak, pathetic loser he must be.* That or the fact Allegra was holding my arm.

Taking out a bar and munching on it would be akin to confirming that I was a loser or something. Some part of me was hoping she understood I needed food for fuel.

Nevertheless, I gritted my teeth, focused on not passing out—which would be the most embarrassing thing ever—and forged on.

I registered neither walking through a door nor sitting at a table. Only when Flame asked about a drink did I regain some lucidity. And when she brought a glass of water to my lips, I downed the lot in two gulps.

"Are your parents here?" I asked as the fog in my head slowly cleared away. When both girls frowned, I added quickly, "Your guardian, I mean."

"Ah, Karma comes around every few weeks or so," Flame said.

It was my turn to frown. "I thought you said her name was Clara."

"I did?" Alex said, still frowning. "Ah, yes. Her real name is Karma." Her hand closed around the pendant around her neck. "I've been trying to reach her for a while now."

"So, you two live alone? Where's your dog?"

"Somewhere. He goes out whenever he wants to."

Alex shrugged and turned to Flame, pointing to her sleeves. The sleeves near her wrists were blackened and frayed.

"Go get changed," she said. Her eyes softened as Flame's head dropped, and she added, "I'll get you another shirt. You did good out there."

Flame hurried up the stairs to what I assumed was her bedroom while Alex checked the fridge. It was an old model with no screen on the door. I shifted and realized that there was nothing inside it.

As I looked around the living room, I noted that the house…was empty too. A few pictures lay on the mantelpiece, the walls were bare, save for a few blackened spots—Flame's doing, no doubt—and all the surfaces were clean.

Suddenly, I missed my home. Every picture, ripped wallpaper, and scratch contained fragments of memory. I finally gave up, fumbled inside my bag, grabbed a bar, and munched on it.

Alex was studying me intently. I held out another bar to her, but she shook her head. My body tensed, and I was on alert again. No shield around my hands, so I reckoned I was safe enough. Still… *Keep your mental barrier up, keep up your mental wall—*

"Relax. I'm not getting inside your mind."

"You just did!"

She scoffed. "Hey, not my fault you're screaming your thoughts. That I can't help hearing. How'd you think I know whenever you think about Flame? It's super annoying."

"So, you can read people's minds and put thoughts into them," I said. "That's your ability, right?" I was hoping she would maybe know a bit more about my power.

"Oh, the mind thing I do is kind of weak."

"Weak?"

"I mean, only a handful of Metas have more than one ability. I happen to be one of them." She rifled through a cupboard. "Sorry, nothing to eat here. We've never had visitors. Come to think of it, you're our first guest." Hands on her hips, she stood in the middle of the kitchen, eyebrows furrowed.

"What's your strongest ability, then?" I asked warily.

Suddenly, she clapped her hands, startling me. "Aha! I knew I had something."

The next few moments made my heart skip. The freezer door flew open, a tub of ice cream flew out, and as the bowl settled on the table, the freezer door closed. Next, a drawer opened. A bowl and a spoon hovered mid-air before settling next to the tub.

"There is no spoon," I murmured as if in a trance. I must be hallucinating.

Alex cast me a glance as if I were the most stupid thing she'd ever laid eyes on. "Of course there's a spoon. What is wrong with you?"

"So you can..."

"Telekinesis. Yeah, I can move stuff around."

I stayed quiet for a long time, watching the scoop dig up ice cream on its own. I couldn't help jumping when the bowl settled on the table in front of me.

"Eat," Alex said. "Rocky Road ice cream; it's all we have. It's Flame's favorite."

Something in her tone made me look up. There was something like pity in her eyes. It seemed she was trying to reach out to me. Given the fact that she's read my mind inadvertently so many times, she had to know I had a crush on her sister. The identical sister she was so protective of. I turned my gaze back to the ice cream b owl.

"She looks so...happy around you. It's been a long time since I've seen her smile. She's usually quiet." When I didn't reply, she added, "Eat up. I know you have a lot of questions. I'll tell you whatever I know, although Karma is the one with all the answers."

I picked up the spoon and took a bite. The cold rein-vigorated me. "You said—you said people with abilities are called Metas. Are there others like us out there?"

"Quite a few. They remain hidden. There are bases around the country to protect them. Both from the hu-mans and from themselves."

I looked at the blackened spots on the walls and nod-ded. "When their abilities are out of control, I'm guess-ing."

Alex sighed and sat across the table. "Yes, Flame's ability. Karma says her blue plasma is unique. But it gets out of control. That's why we left the last orphanage we lived in. She almost burned the whole building down. Then Karma came to us."

"Why can't she live at a base and train there? Learn to control the blue sparks—uh, plasma thing."

"Karma says that training can't teach her that. Flame can get...emotional. Too emotional. Emotions affect her ability to control it."

I didn't know what to say, so I ate more ice cream. Telling her about the connection I felt was probably not the right time.

"So why did you come here, to Golden Birch? Why did you enroll at the school? And...wait, you said you came to my rescue because of the mark on my hand."

"Yes, Karma saw you in one of her visions, but lately, they've been very confusing. She sent us on a mission to find the Meta with the blue shield."

"Visions? The future or the past?" I suddenly shook my head. "Wait, it can't be me. My shield is red."

"I know it's red. She first saw you in a lab being experimented on, but you had no mark back then. Then, you fell from a building."

"I've never been in a lab." I paused, spoon midway to my mouth. "But I did fall off a building three days ago. That's when the mark appeared."

Alex took off one fingerless glove and held out her hand, palm down. The mark was similar to mine, with a triangle inside a circle. But where mine had a small cross inside the triangle, hers had two connected circles like an infinity sign. My eyes widened. The computers at Westview had shown the same mark.

"Does Flame have one too? Do you know what they mean?"

"Flame doesn't, and Karma is trying to locate others with the mark."

"So, the mark makes us special or something? Why doesn't Flame have one if she's so powerful?"

"I'm glad she doesn't." Alex gritted her teeth. "That mark is a damn curse. Karma is a powerful mage, maybe even the most powerful of all. Yet, she looked so scared when she saw the mark on my hand. She came to us a few months ago, days after my mark appeared. I've been trying to find out what it means since. Karma never told me, but I'm certain she knows something about it." She wrapped her hand around the hourglass-shaped pendant around her neck.

I nodded toward it. "Cool pendant."

She hummed. "It's how I call Karma. But she hasn't answered any of my calls. I guess she must be in one of her deep meditation sessions. She does that a lot. For the visions."

"Maybe you can leave a voicemail or something?"

Alex threw me one of her how-are-you-so-stupid glares. I swallowed, and my gaze drifted to the stairs. I wished Flame would hurry up.

"What's next?"

"We wait until Karma contacts me. My mission was to find you and keep you safe." Suddenly, she turned around toward the doorway, and I followed her gaze. "Tommy, has Karma contacted you?"

As I peered through the doorway, a figure in front of a laptop shifted. His head turned toward us, eyes blank. It almost made me uncomfortable—I hadn't even sensed anyone nearby. I caught a glimpse of the laptop screen, black with white text. Coding or hacking, most likely. I'd only seen it in movies, but the speed at which the numbers ran baffled me. How was the boy called Tommy able to process everything? I figured he was around the same age as us, too. Strange.

"Hold on," I said, recognizing the familiar black hair and dark eyes. "I saw you a few days ago at school. You were following Alex, right?" I turned to her. "Is he your brother?"

The boy lifted his hand and gave a small wave.

"No contact with Karma yet," he said, and his gaze fell on me as if he'd just noticed I was there. "Hello, Michael Jacobs. It's...nice to meet you."

"Uh, yeah, nice to meet you, too. What are you doing over there?"

"Leave him be," Alex interrupted. "He's busy right now. Tommy, don't mind us. Just continue working." Tommy complied, eyes fixated on his screen again.

"I wonder how the Tracker caught onto you so fast. You said the mark appeared when you fell from the building three days ago, right?"

"The morning after, actually. Maybe it was the Precog?"

"Nah, Precogs can see only a few hours ahead."

Anger surged inside me. Because of them, I had to leave my home. Because of them, my life was upturned, and I couldn't go back to school.

Alex's eyes narrowed. "You're hiding something. You knew you were being followed and packed a bag to run away. How did *you* know about the Trackers?"

"I saw one of them. The one who keeps sniffing and has a mole. It's like an image that popped into my mind, and I guess I just knew he was after me. They wanted me to meet someone called Commander Rimes."

"So, you have two abilities like me... Wait! How did Rimes find out about you so quickly *and* send the Trackers?"

"Did I say Rimes? No, I meant—" Suddenly, a warm tendril crossed my mind, and I froze. "Get out of my head!"

"It's important!" Alex protested. "How do you know about Rimes? My mission was to find you before he does and keep you safe from him."

I held out my index finger. "Give me a minute, will you?" I tried to gather my thoughts about everything that happened in the last few days. My trips to Westview, the encounter with the cultists, and the Trackers. There was too much information, and I didn't know where to start.

"Who were those two people with you at the park?" I asked.

Alex startled. "You saw them?"

"I was there when they attacked you and Flame. They had something that blocked my shield."

"It's called a nullifier. Flame and I were both power-less."

I recalled the incident. Flame staring at the men with defiant eyes, blue sparks on the ground, the silver tube in the man's palm.

"It doesn't explain how you know about Rimes and him about you," Alex said. She was practically growling like a lioness. "Are you working with him?"

"I was getting to that. And no! Of course—why would I work—ugh, never mind. Look, I've just been hanging out in the Westview building a lot lately. You know, the old, creepy abandoned hospital?" Alex only stared back, arms crossed. "Okay, okay, um. So, I was there at the hospital last night when a lot of military trucks showed up. They had equipment, computers, satellites, guns, you name it. I only managed to get out because I recognized a soldier there. Someone I knew from the orphanage I lived in. He tried to protect me when his superior turned up. She mentioned the name 'Rimes.'"

But Alex was still frowning when I looked up. "And the two men who attacked us?"

"They were at the building too. And they were chanting about this...Aequus. I thought it was a cult group or something."

"Aequus... Karma's mentioned that name before. Other than the mark, it's the only other thing that seems to scare her... And for someone with so much power to be afraid..."

"You look up to her a lot."

"She got me and Flame out of the orphanage. But she... she, I don't know, sometimes sees power where people are. Flame has more power than I do, and that takes priority."

Alex's eyes softened again. I knew how siblings often looked at each other, seen it in other kids at school: anger, jealousy, resentment, pure annoyance. But in Alex, there was no such thing; she really loved her twin sister to bits.

"Like I said, Karma's a Mage; from the little I understand, her kind lives for millennia. She's on our side, you know. She trusts me enough to fulfill this mission of finding others with our mark."

Her voice was filled with reverence. Was it any different from the cult I'd witnessed the previous night? "And you trust her, too," I said warily. "She must have her own reasons for getting you two involved. Two teen girls against a horde of soldiers under Commander Rimes? That's not right."

Alex frowned and straightened. "Flame and I can take care of ourselves."

"From what I saw yesterday morning, you were both out of your league with that nullifier." I regretted my words as soon as they were out of my mouth. Who was I to tell them what they could do? But I hated the thought that this Karma was putting them at risk. Flame at risk. And for what?

"If I hadn't knocked those two men out," I continued, "there's no telling what could've happened."

A shriek made me jump, and I dropped my spoon on the table. Ice cream splattered across the marble in black and white blobs.

"That was you, Michael? You rescued us?" Flame called out, her voice high-pitched. "I thought I saw a red flash across the sky. Didn't I tell you? I told you, Ash!"

"Who's Ash?"

"She's right here, silly. My sister!" Flame skipped over to the kitchen counter, took out a bowl, and scooped up a double serving of ice cream.

"You'll have to taste the ice cream at the Waffle

House," I said with a smile. I glanced down at her hands. She didn't have a mark. "The servings are huge. Plus, you get unlimited toppings."

"Really? Wow!" Flame sent me a beaming smile while Alex—ugh, Ash (if only they could just stick to one name, dammit) rolled her eyes. My smile faltered as I realized I was asking her out. Not on a date or anything, but an invitation. Of sorts. I mean, it was too soon, and we barely—

"Ah, shut it," Ash said, groaning. "Some thoughts are fuzzy, and I can block them out. But yours are just... Eugh." She made a gagging sound that set my face on fire. "I need to change, anyway." She spun around and climbed up the stairs.

Considering Mole-Man could still be tracking my scent, I should also have a good wash. Flame threw a kitchen towel at me, so I cleaned up the mess at the table. She brought her bowl over and sat down.

"I heard about your friend Ben. You don't seem to have any friends at school. Other than Jack and Kyle." Her eyes twinkled, and I realized she'd probably been eavesdropping from upstairs. The thought made me flush.

For an unexplained reason, I felt completely relaxed. "Ben and I were at the orphanage together seven years ago. He got adopted first, and then the Jacobs adopted me months later. I haven't seen him since then. Until last night, of course."

"But you said he protected you."

My eyebrows furrowed. "The soldiers came to the hospital and were searching for intruders. He hid me while his superior questioned him."

"You think he's in trouble?"

"I think she knew he was hiding someone, so yes." I couldn't help the guilt surging inside me. I'd been telling myself that Ben would be okay when I knew very well he wouldn't be. "I also heard another voice," I blurted out.

It was too late to wonder whether it was okay for me to be saying all these things.

"Like Ash's voice?"

"No, but it was definitely a telepathic voice. There was no one else close by. It was asking—begging—for my help. But I didn't have time to find out who it was."

Flame didn't say anything. Her eyes grew distant as she took small bites of the ice cream. "Did Ash tell you about the recent Meta disappearances? We've been trying to locate Opal's base for some time."

"Opal?"

"Black Opal. That's what Rimes' group is called. Maybe he's keeping them at the Westview building. That would make sense. Lots of medical supplies. Deserted place. Plenty of rooms. Easy to secure exits."

"I don't think the site is safe. My shield is always up

when I'm there." Obviously because of the sinkhole. Was I really that stupid?

"You were training?" Flame smiled. She had bits of dark cookie pieces stuck between her front teeth, and it made her look like the most adorable thing I've ever set eyes on. "We should practice together sometime. My sparks versus your shield."

"Sounds like a promise."

"I don't hold back," she said sheepishly, pointing at the blackened streaks on the wallpaper behind me.

I smiled. "Wouldn't want you to."

Before I knew it, it was already past four. To be perfectly honest, it had been such a long time since I felt so comfortable around someone. Flame and I chatted like long-lost friends. When I pointed at Tommy, still staring intensely at the old laptop, Flame assured me he was fine. I wondered what kind of stuff he was working on. Clearly, he was trying to hack into something.

I was surprised to see Ash leave us be. She picked up an old book—which I noted to be ancient history, my least favorite subject—and sat in a corner, fidgeting with the hourglass pendant.

"History?" I asked.

"Yeah, there's so much to learn!" Ash said, her eyes bright. I was surprised to see her so excited. She was usually cool and disinterested. "The few snippets I gathered from Karma and my research led to the Sumer. A similar mark to ours was engraved on a headstone on the site."

"Sumer? Isn't that from like thousands of years ago?"

"Yep, about eight thousand, actually. Sumerians called themselves the 'black-headed people,' did you know that? Karma says Etana, one of the kings, was a Meta. He was 'the shepherd who ascended to heaven.' He could fly, basically."

"Uh, you know that for sure? I mean, history is a bit, uh, vague." I'd rather place my trust in science. History was the bane of my life. Then again, there was too much that science couldn't explain now.

"History is what makes us," Ash said tensely. Her eyes widened, bright and alive. "And we have to learn from it." I nodded, but maybe something told her I wasn't that convinced.

"Have you heard the epic of Gilgamesh?"

"It's a story, right? A fictional story? Yeah." I kept nodding at her, even though I didn't have a single clue what she was on about. She turned away, and I sighed in relief.

"Hey, did you know the Sumerians had pyramids like the Mayans and Egyptians?" Ash said. I inwardly groaned. "Or that the Hungarian language is close to the Sumerians'? Perhaps these abilities were meant to unite the world, prevent wars, stuff like that."

"So, you're saying our abilities are hidden in our genes until something happens that makes them flare up? That still doesn't explain why we have the mark, and Flame doesn't."

"Maybe we're descendants of these people," she said thoughtfully. "Descendants, or genetically modified, I don't know. I mean, the Mages have natural powers, so maybe it isn't genetic modification." Her speech grew faster as she continued, and I struggled to keep up. "But we know several Sumerian artifacts disappeared from museums and collections throughout the world. Some of these artifacts are even sentient and can choose who uses them. Black Opal has some of them." She lets out a wry laugh. "Not that that's common knowledge, obviously."

"Is that why Opal's kidnapping Metas? To find the marked ones?"

"Karma thinks they already have their hands on a couple of them. Years ago, Karma tracked two teens with the mark and came close to finding them, but they disappeared soon after. She's certain they're still alive. What's worse is that she thinks they might be working for Opal. Rimes would probably keep them close by. If we could find their base, where they're taking the Metas... maybe we can persuade them to join our side and help us." She thought for a moment, then shook her head. "I didn't even believe Karma at first. Metas helping Opal? It doesn't make sense. But she said we have to consider every possibility."

I remained silent. I had no such optimism. I was thinking more about the kind of movies where the mutants were persecuted for being different, soldiers running after the genetically modified, and scientists experimenting on them.

Flame interrupted the contemplative silence to complain about being hungry, so Ash quickly put her books away. When I offered to help get groceries, both girls shook their heads. Tim, the Mole-Man, might still be lurking around. The girls claimed they'd quickly get to the grocery store and be back soon. They assured me that Rimes' men couldn't get through the charm this house was supposedly under.

My instincts, on the other hand, were warning me. And I was right. After they left, everything became a mess.

My eyes flew open, and I sat up. I must've nodded off while Ash and Flame were away. The house was quiet. I listened, unsure of what woke me up. Tommy sat at the table, his head resting on his arms.

My body was on full alert, tendrils of red swirling around my hands. I recognized the sense of dread coursing through me. The same dread I felt when Flame and Ash were under attack at Broadway Park.

But this time, the two girls were safe. I had no clue how I knew that, but I did.

I slowly got off the sofa. I had to move. Somewhere, anywhere. Ah, yes, Westview Hospital. I grabbed my coat and slipped my shoes and bag on. But what was it—

Then the image crossed my mind, and I froze mid-step.

It couldn't be. My breath caught in my throat.

But why?

Then, I was on the move. I ripped the door open and ran. I didn't stop until the dark outline of the crooked building appeared in my line of sight.

He'll come.

How can you be sure?

As sure as I am of our victory.

The swirls around my hands thickened as I drew near the building. But I wouldn't—couldn't—stay away.

Strangely, there was no one patrolling the front gate. That should've been my cue to stay away. But, stubborn as I was, I forged ahead.

That was when I saw Ben standing in the middle

of the path. My first thought was that he looked well enough. Then, as I peered closer at his outline in the encroaching darkness, I realized something wasn't quite right.

I braced myself.

"He was sure you'd come," Ben said in an even tone. "Why did you?"

"I—Did they beat you up?" I asked, my voice trembling as I spoke.

Ben chuckled. "I'm here as bait. Or maybe I'm here to persuade you to join our side."

"Ben—" He didn't answer my question. No, something was wrong. Something was really wrong.

He raised his hand and coughed. A dark, thick liquid spluttered out of his mouth. "Whatever you have to say, save it. You shouldn't have come. You shouldn't—" Another cough racked his body, and he staggered.

"They know everything. They knew you'd come. They know you were here before. They know we know each other. They even knew you'd know about the beating."

He was slurring, and something in his eyes sent a shiver down my spine.

"Ben, I can help you," I started. "Come with me. We'll leave together. Somewhere far away. Somewhere safe."

I knew I was sounding desperate. The light was shifting, and I saw his eyes clearly. I recognized that look.

Someone who knew he was condemned and was re-signed to it because he had no way out. A young boy on death row.

I tensed, a shiver running down my spine. I didn't wait for anything to happen. I burst a shield from my hands, sensing someone was watching. Sure enough, I spotted soldiers running in formation toward us. I pulled the shield around us further and seized Ben's hand. He didn't budge.

No. Not like this.

"They'll find you, Michael," Ben said quietly. "No mat-ter where you run to. I... I always knew you'd be someone very, very important. You always looked out for the little guys." A small smile spread across his bloodied lips. Then he took a deep breath as if bracing himself. "But not me. I just looked after me. So run away, friend, far away from these people. They're determined to get you, to have you on their side. Don't ever let them get their filthy hands on you. Don't...don't let them brainwash you." His voice rose, yet I stood still, frozen in place. "Go! Do it for me, please! Run! Far from here! Go!"

His last words were so loud that I jumped and let go of his hand as I stepped away. The sound echoed in the empty front yard. Still, I didn't run. It was as if my mind couldn't comprehend his words. The soldiers could have nullifiers on them, and I braced myself.

Suddenly, my red shield disappeared, and I froze, knowing what came next.

A gunshot sounded.

Ben staggered to the side. A dark splatter appeared, barely visible on the front of his green camo. I should've done something. Moved. The nullifier made me feel weak and powerless. I clenched my fists, but as he collapsed, I took another step back. His glassy eyes seemed to be staring at me, widened. His words echoed in my mind, but I couldn't move. I was still frozen on the spot, and the soldiers were moving in on me. One was prepping a dart gun.

The thudding of footsteps sounded behind me. I snapped back into focus.

"Michael!" I looked up. Blue sparks flew above my head toward the soldiers. Flame. How far away she was, I didn't know. But it was close enough for the plasma to rain down on the soldiers, who retreated. The nullifiers were scorched, and my red waves returned.

Ash grabbed onto my arm as I reached out toward Ben. "We have to leave," she said quickly, her eyes sparing Ben a brief, pitying glance. "Flame?"

"More soldiers coming our way. I can take out two or three of them at a time, but there are too many."

"I can't hold off their weapons for long," Ash said quickly, her voice bordering on panic. "Let's go!" When I didn't move, she said with more force. "You heard your friend. They want your power. They used him as bait. Come back with us." She paused, weighing her following words for a split second. "Do it for him."

As if in a trance, I nodded. Then, all three of us ran.

CHAPTER 15

Day 4, night

"How did you find me?" I asked when we reached Broadview Park. It took me a few moments to catch my breath from running all the way from West-view Hospital. Ash stood before me, arms crossed and eyebrows furrowed, while Flame sat on the bench. She cast me a glance, and I glimpsed the hurt in her eyes. She looked away quickly, flicking little blue plasma balls from hand to hand. In the darkness surrounding us, they glowed faintly.

I didn't care much for Ash's anger, but Flame's sadness sent a little pang of guilt through my heart. *Why did you leave?*

I wished I could explain, but I could only think of Ben. His glassy eyes. The dark liquid sputtering out of his mouth. In my dream, soldiers were beating him up. But to kill him...to use him as bait... They'd been so sure I'd turn up. All this just to get to me.

"You left," Ash stated firmly.

"I had a dream." My voice was hoarse as the images roiled in my head. "I saw Ben. They were beating him. I thought I could save him..."

Flame still didn't look at me. Her silent treatment hurt more than I expected.

"I'm sorry your friend's dead," Ash said, and her voice grew softer for a moment. She touched my shoulder gently, then sighed. "But now, you understand what we're up against. These are cold-blooded killers."

"Why? Why me? Why this damn mark? I want nothing to do with it!" I started rubbing the back of my hand even though I knew it was useless. The skin turned red and raw from the friction, but all I could see were Ben's lifeless eyes. "They'd kill for this thing?"

"I don't know why they're after us. Karma knows, but she hasn't contacted me yet." Something like hesitation crept into her voice before disappearing. "I'll bring you to a base. You'll be safer there than wandering the streets. They know who you are now, and it's only a matter of time until their Trackers find you again."

"I thought you trusted us," Flame said. Her voice was so quiet that I thought it was the breeze blowing past us.

"I do," I said quickly. "I still do. I trust you both. It's just these visions. I can't explain any of them. Like when I knew those men were in the park and you were under attack, and now with Ben...I couldn't...I mean, to leave him behind..." *What was the point of it all? You did all of that, and Ben's still gone. You couldn't save him.*

The blue plasma in Flame's hand sparked bright for a moment, then faded. "I understand," she said quietly. "I'm sorry. I promise I'm not mad." She gave me a small, wilting smile. "And I'm sorry about your friend, too."

Ash cleared her throat, half-startling me. Great. Oh, so great. I narrowed my eyes at her. But before I could protest, she shrugged and said, "Hey, not my fault. Like I said, I pick up on your thoughts about Flame."

She rolled her eyes as Flame beamed a smile at me. Looked like my sudden disappearance was forgiven. I sent a mental thank-you to Ash but wasn't sure if it reached her.

I gave her a nod and swallowed hard before turning to Ash. "So, what do we do now? Go hide in a base and wait for Karma to contact me?" I couldn't help the bitterness in my voice.

"Let's talk about your powers," Ash said.

"What about them?" I froze. "Is it because of what happened..." I stopped short. Even though there was no logic to it, I couldn't help feeling guilty. Did Ben die because of me? Did he die because I couldn't react any faster? *If you'd reacted faster, Ben wouldn't have died. You're not good enough. You let him die. Without Ash and Flame, you'd be in Rimes' hands by now. Maybe you deserve to be. Useless. Pathetic.*

As if reading my mind, Flame said, "It's not your fault." She reached out for my hand and took it gently.

It was as if a dam broke inside me. When someone is being nice, and you're right there at the bottom, it really breaks you. I started shaking. *Don't cry…don't cry.* I tensed my body, but it was no use.

"Oh, just cry and get it out," Ash said with a soft sigh. "Seriously, there's no point in holding it back."

Being close to a telepath was so frustrating. I clenched my fists and took a deep breath to calm myself down. "Now that I'm on the run, should I go by Michael, or can I choose a fake name, too?" It felt good to change the subject, even though my voice was slightly choked.

"Do I look like an Allegra?" Flame said thoughtfully. I shook my head.

"Karma will know your real name," Ash said. "And if you want to know how we tracked you, Flame's the one to thank. She said you mentioned Westview and hearing voices. So, we thought you might go back there. What we didn't expect was that Opal set a trap for you. With your friend as bait."

"I didn't sense anyone else there," Flame said, then turned to me quickly. "None of the kidnapped Metas. Metas have a special bioelectric field. But I only sensed the soldiers."

"But how did they know?" Ash said. "How did they know you'd come?"

Bioelectric? Sensed? I shrugged. "Do I get to choose a new name or not?" I asked, suddenly eager to change the conversation again.

Ash huffed in annoyance. "Yeah, you can if you want to. You've got to give everything up, anyway. There's no going back. Once Black Opal is onto you, there's nothing you can do except run. Let's get you to the base. It's in the forest north of Golden Birch."

"Everwood Forest?"

"I don't have a map. But yes." Ash picked up her bag, and Flame followed suit.

"Flame says you've been trying to find the kidnapped Metas," I said. "But why does Opal take them? For what purpose?"

"Opal's minions don't know much," Ash answered as we began walking. "Since they bring the kidnapped kids to scientists, there's only one conclusion to draw from that."

"And you'd be one of the kids if I hadn't turned up yesterday morning. "A grim silence settled over the group until Ash suddenly spoke up again.

"Hang on. How did your shield manifest next to a nullifier? Are you immune to it or something?"

"Oh, no," I said quickly. "But I also noticed my shield

disappeared when I was within a certain distance. Maybe fifty to seventy meters. So, the thing has a limited range, and I was pretty sure I could throw my shield and take them out from afar."

She hummed thoughtfully. "Good. Now we know its weakness."

Flame continued juggling the blue plasma balls between her hands and spinning them between her fingers as we walked. I was following close behind as we crossed the open space. I felt very exposed, but the girls seemed confident that there was no one else but us.

Suddenly, I bumped into Flame, and she dropped one of the balls. A hiss sounded, and I noticed wisps of smoke rising from the scorched grass. I stared at the blackened spot while Flame uttered a sheepish apology.

Damn, damn, damn. What was I getting myself into? Did I have any choice other than to follow these two? I looked up at Flame. A lamp pole cast light into her hazel eyes. Her blush was so enticing and...

I shook my head. Things were moving too fast. My gaze went back to the scorched grass. Metas who were out of control could do real damage.

The ball that bounced off my shield and hit Jack was unintentional. The rock that hit Zachary on the shoulder—also unintended. It could've been much worse. If I'd angled it differently, if I'd used more force... I could've killed them both. Honestly, I could've gotten myself killed too.

Heck, I could do real damage with my shield if I didn't learn to control it. What if some random passerby saw me using my powers?

"Ordinary people can't see our abilities," Ash said, sensing my doubts. "Only other Metas." She stopped in her tracks and met my gaze. "Michael, understand your parents are in danger. It's best to leave and come with us to keep them safe. My mission is to find the ones with the mark and protect them. Flame and I are on your side—you do know that, right?" She turned on her heel and resumed walking without waiting for my reply.

"I didn't get a chance to say goodbye," I started. "My foster parents, I mean." I shrugged and then winced. Janet loathed these "whatever" shrugs. A painful ache grew in my chest. I might never see Janet or Mark again. They'd taught me so much. I gritted my teeth, regret and anger filling every bone in my body.

"Ditch your phone," Ash continued. "No point in contacting them."

Deep down inside, I knew Ash was right. To keep them safe, I had to leave town. Was it forever or until Black Opal stopped chasing us? But I knew they weren't giving up. They knew where I lived and could use the Jacobs as leverage against me. The only way to protect them was to show them I didn't care about the Jacobs.

I swallowed the lump in my throat and hurried to catch up to Ash and Flame. I'd always lived in Golden Birch. So, leaving felt so...permanent.

Ash continued, "You can safely train and learn to harness your powers at the base. Some Metas have hurt their loved ones. It takes effort to control your powers. Just...think of it as a vacation week. Stay at the base until I get news from Karma."

"Karma again," I muttered. Despite everything, I felt like challenging Ash. Call it denial, anger or pure resentment, but some part of me didn't want to follow her, even if it was for my safety.

"Karma is a powerful Mage," Ash answered in a matter-of-fact tone as if she hadn't said it a thousand times before. As if that explained everything. Metas? Mages? What was next? Dragons? Dwarfs? She rubbed her cheek, lost in thought. I wondered for a split second if my thoughts were too loud for her. Well, whatever.

"Karma's a Precog, too," Flame added from a distance. "Well, she knows about prophecies. Her Precog abilities aren't as good. She does have visions of the future, though. But sometimes, they're fuzzy. She saw your mark months ago, but there were no specifics. Just that you were in Golden Birch."

"Months ago?" I repeated.

"Yeah, Rimes' Precogs can be easily fooled," Flame said. "They know only the near future, like a few hours or minutes, and even then, their visions aren't accurate at all. Karma also sees possibilities, and her visions are much more accurate. Then there are the Postcogs, the ones who can see the past. Those are rare. Karma is tracking a Postcog right now. She's supposed to be marked like us, but she's very elusive. A powerful Postcog might tell us how your marks came to be and more about the past." Flame hugged her arms to herself and slowed her pace slightly. "You know—it's just something I've been feeling for a while. But something is coming."

Her tone was so low when she said the last few words that I almost didn't catch them. But the flicker of fear in her eyes was clear. Again, we fell into silence until Ash broke it.

"So, Michael, what else can you do?" Ash asked. "Other than the shield, that is. You said you heard voices and had dreams that were visions."

I looked down at my hands. Sadly, not a single wave of energy flickered around them. The silver lining was I must be very safe next to Ash and Flame.

"Why bother asking when you can just read my mind?" I asked, rolling my eyes in disdain.

"It's called respecting your privacy," she countered. "Most of the time, I tune everyone out. It can get overwhelming, all the noise. I have my own rules: don't go through people's minds unless they're the enemy or it's absolutely necessary."

"Being telekinetic and telepathic is more powerful than manifesting a shield," I said slowly. Back at Westview, she was keeping the soldiers from firing at me.

A dry leaf floated up and stayed there, hovering at eye level. I gulped. Physics dictated that no matter how small an object, it could be deadly when traveling fast.

"You can move things too," Ash said. "Like when you tossed Tim, the sniffer, away."

"Yes, I mean, no. I can't move things. I can only defend myself and move things attacking me using my shield. Like rocks. And people."

"Interesting... so how did you know Tim was a danger? Did you have a read on him?" I shrugged, but Ash wasn't going to be dismissed so easily. "I saw you in the parking lot at the mall. You had a look of recognition on your face when you saw him. That meant you'd seen him before, right?"

"You followed me?"

"Calm down. I knew you were trying to ditch us, and we were on our way home when we saw the Trackers. Wait. Your dreams! I wonder..."

Suddenly, Ash's eyes widened. Not in joy, but as one would when making a discovery while examining a bug under a microscope.

"I had a vision of Mole—uh, Tim," I said quickly. "At first, it was just his mole with a whisker." Ash's nose wrinkled. "Gross, I know. I was by Westview when I first had a vision, and he sniffed a lot."

"I don't think you're a Precog."

"Yeah, I didn't do too well in that fight."

"I think what you have is coeval cognizance," Ash said, ignoring me. "It's even rarer than Precogs and Postcogs."

"Evil what?"

"Coeval." For her fourteen years, Ash had such a big vocabulary. Flame was watching me in amusement, and I shook my head. She knew much more about Metas than I did, and it seemed she was using common terms. I wouldn't know.

Ash continued, "It just means that you're aware of events happening in the present regardless of space. Karma can tell us more about your ability. If only she'd answer my calls! I've been summoning her for days."

Summoning. It sounded like I was in a fantasy world with mages, witches, and magic. Together with guns, soldiers, and assault rifles. All that stuff was fine in movies, yet the reality wasn't nearly as glamorous.

I noticed we were finally out of the park and headed toward the industrial part of Golden Birch. On a Thursday night, all the streets were deserted.

"Have you ever had any weird dreams? Of monsters?" Ash asked suddenly.

Her insistence bothered me. I wasn't about to tell nosy Ash about my dream of a dragon-like monster snoozing with a red net on its back. The recurring dream—nightmare—had me waking up in the middle of the night soaked in sweat.

But nobody knew about this, not even Janet. How did one shield their thoughts from a mind-reader? I wasn't ready to share this with anyone, but I gritted my teeth. "How did you know?"

"No mind-reading, I swear. Karma said you might know something about a monster. It's after you, the Child Protector."

Child? I wasn't a child. Before I could ask for more, Flame rushed toward us, her eyes bright. I noticed her blue balls of energy plasma were bouncing and growing bigger by the second. I took a careful step back. The air sizzled in the clearing like a storm was approaching.

"Hey," Flame chimed in, "We've got to move faster. I just read four Opal agents on the street behind us. They'll have the Precogs all over us in seconds."

"Read?" I swallowed. Was Flame a mind-reader too? She'd know about my crush and—

"Yep," she simply said, looking down at the glowing blue balls in her hands. Longingly and lovingly. "That's my power: this lovely little plasma. But I can also read heat signatures, too."

Ah, the bioelectric fields. I thought of mentioning electrocuting and scorching, but left the words hanging.

Ash picked up the pace, nearly jogging in her haste. I sighed and lined up after her. Flame walked by my side this time. Body heat signatures. Now I understood why Ash used her as a scout, and she always led the way.

Flame suddenly looked at me sideways, her head lowered and said, "I love your bioelectric field," she said shyly.

"My bio... uh, thanks?"

"It's unique to every individual, like a fingerprint or brain waves. I can identify shapeshifters this way." She looked proud. "Your field is so...magnetic. It's beautiful."

She stepped back as if she'd said too much. I remembered how mesmerized I was watching the blue sparks in the courtyard.

"I love your blue...sparks too. They're, uh... *electrifying*."

Her shyness disappeared as her wide smile returned. I smiled back. My breaths quickened. At this rate, the brisk walk combined with her smile was going to knock me out. But before I could say anything else, Flame moved away to join Ash in front of me.

For the first time, I felt that I belonged somewhere. She seemed to have that effect on me. The feeling of home.

Yet, these two girls were strangers until a few hours ago. Living alone in an abandoned and soon-to-be-destroyed building wasn't appealing. But with Trackers on my heels, there was nowhere to hide.

Then, there was some part of me that trusted the two girls: one who could blast plasma energy from her fingertips and burn down the city and the other who could read my mind and whip objects at my face whenever she felt like it.

Well, they'd rescued my puny life twice in the span of a few hours, first from Mole-Man, then from Rimes. I didn't have much of a choice, but between Opal and two girls who could help me find answers, I'd choose the latter.

"Here we go," I said, even as hesitation washed into my thoughts like a giant wave. The girls waved back without looking. Ugh. They were so confident that I'd follow, and they were right. I struggled to catch up with my heavy backpack.

In the past few hours, I'd had the longest conversations in my entire life. It almost felt as if I'd made two friends. Almost. And that was a first in a long time.

CHAPTER 16

You'd think a teenager walking with a beautiful girl (I didn't count Ash, who was throwing me annoyed stares and side-eyeing me) alone at night would be such a perfect setting for a date. Romantic, even. Unfortunately, that wasn't the case.

"Are you sure we aren't being followed?" I asked for the gazillionth time.

We were still crossing the northern part of Golden Birch and heading toward Everwood Forest.

Flame rolled her eyes at me. "Relax. A few security guards are patrolling the warehouses, and some workers taking the night shift are about, but we're fine. We've put enough distance between us and the Opal agents by now."

I flexed my wrists, red tendrils swirling around my fingers. "But my shield appears when danger is close by. And it's never been wrong." Something wasn't quite right, but Ash and Flame were still at ease.

Ash glanced at my hands. "So, you can't manifest

them at will, then?"

I shook my head and glanced around. We'd reached the outskirts of Golden Birch with run-down buildings and empty streets. High-rise complexes, blotting out the skyline, loomed over us. Scraggly bushes dotted the pavement. Unlike the west end, these houses looked abandoned and deserted. I recognized the general zone—I'd been here a couple of times since patrol bots didn't regularly scan abandoned areas—but the memory of Ben arose, too. We used to hide here together.

I shook the thought from my head and focused on examining the area. One of the houses looked as if it were ready to keel over, with a hole in the roof and long weeds lining a stone path that was cracked from erosion. I shuddered, wondering how long it had been since anyone had been there. Most of the houses looked the same as we were nearing closer to the forest—they must have been abandoned for a long time.

"Your mana is way down," Ash said suddenly, interrupting my thoughts and pointing to my forearm.

That was when I noticed a shimmering line running from my wrist to my elbow. Well, that hadn't been there before. "Mana?"

"Energy levels."

Huh. I'd been measuring this mana stuff by the hunger pangs gnawing at my stomach. Ash must have heard the growling as she motioned toward a bus stand. We all sat on the bench and shared a packet of Cheetos and peanuts. Sure enough, when I twisted my forearm, the shimmering line had notched higher up to my elbow. Cool.

A few Cheetos and peanuts made for a meager dinner. My decision crisis was whether I should dig in my rations stuffed inside my bag or not. This hadn't been a problem when I was on the streets, but now I was a growing teen with a power that drained my energy every time I used it. I really hoped that whatever safe base we were heading to would have a good stock of food.

I peered at my elbow and the shimmering line. It was steady. I wondered how high it had climbed after my enormous breakfast the day before. Just moments earlier, the line had been so low. What would happen if it vanished? Would that mean I was dead?

The thought dampened my spirits. I was in unchartered territory here, not knowing when my next meal would be, not knowing when Black Opal would catch up to me. I'd probably never have a good breakfast again. Nor would I see my foster parents.

Flame threw me a glance filled with concern. She seemed to feel my dejection, almost as if we were tuned in to each other. Or was my face an open book showing how miserable I felt? Gosh, I hoped she wasn't an empath.

I tried to give her a reassuring smile but failed. I couldn't bring myself to smile or even make small talk.

I stood up and glanced around. The area around us wasn't as well maintained as the eastern end where I lived. Well, used to. I took a closer look. No one was around for sure, or Flame would've alerted us to a heat signature.

Yet, I couldn't help the feeling of being watched.

"Let's move," I said. "This part of town's not safe." Safety these days was relative. A thought struck me. "You've seen Commander Rimes before, haven't you?"

Ash shuddered. "You do *not* want to meet him."

"I think I already have, sort of. Guy with a scar on his forehead and a prosthetic leg that makes a clopping noise when he walks."

Ash looked panic-stricken. "Has he seen you? He must've. He knows what you look like. There would've been cameras when you sneaked into Westview."

"You asked how he knew I'd come. Now I remember. I was in a dream watching Ben getting beaten. Then Rimes turned and looked straight at me. He knew I was there. He knew I'd come for Ben."

"I don't know about Rimes' powers. Could be he's watching us right now, for all I know. I've read something peculiar in one of his minions' minds. They're afraid of someone called SB. Someone who could travel through time and space."

"Woah. So, SB could probably see us right here and right now. Damn, they could even see *where* we're going to go."

Flame stuck out her tongue toward the sky. "Bet they can see me doing this right now." I stifled a snort of laughter, and she looked rather pleased with herself.

Ash rolled her eyes at us and shrugged. "Whoever SB is, they can't be more powerful than Karma. Finding the right path for the future takes a lot of time. I mean, she saw you with a blue shield instead of a red one, but she was still pretty accurate. Bet SB couldn't do all that." She shrugged. "Let's take the bus. It goes around the forest. It's a longer route, and the end of the line is on the other side of the forest. That way, we won't have to walk the entire way."

"But we'll get there quicker if we cut across," Flame said. She stood up and did a little skip. "I'd love to see the forest. Never been in one before."

Ash folded her arms. "Yeah, because we want to avoid a forest fire."

Flame hung her head in disappointment. Clearly, she was looking forward to this new experience. Ash must've coddled her a lot if she was so curious about the world that she was willing to enter the forest at night. Unease ran through me at the thought. Not that I was afraid of the dark, but the red tendrils around my hands refused to disappear.

"Is there another route?" I asked, then nodded toward the line of trees. "Are there any animals in there?"

Ash shrugged again. "Mountain lions, wolves, bears, and more, from what I've heard. Nothing that we can't handle, but still. I think we should take the long route." She glanced over at Flame. "Y'know, the *safe* route."

"And add another two hours to the trip?" Flame said to my dismay. "I'd rather cut across. Plus, we can't stay on the roads. That's where Opal will be looking for us."

Nothing seemed to faze her. And she *did* have a point. My respect for her rose a notch. I stood, flanked by the two sisters who stared at me. Evidently, they were expecting me to act as the tiebreaker on this vote. Taking the long road would make me look like a wimp. But it was the safest.

My phone vibrated with an incoming text. Avoiding Alex's eyes, I checked it quickly. It was Janet. My heart ached, filled with sadness. How do I say goodbye?

Hey, haven't heard from you or the babysitter lately. Is the house still standing?

Well, we had two intruders, one who kept sniffing and the other who could see the future. Other than that, the house was in tip-top shape. It was still standing to answer the question. So I texted Janet, 'All good!' with lots of smiling emojis.

And note to myself: warn the babysitter. I quickly texted the latter next that I'd picked up a virus from school and needed to recover, along with some premature reassurance that I already had medicine and everything I needed and that she wouldn't need to check up on me. With any luck, she wouldn't show up after that.

"You'll have to ditch your folks," Ash said, looking annoyed, "and that phone."

Easier said than done. I clenched my fists and wished she'd shut up. "Will do," I muttered.

She continued, "It's for their their safety. The sooner you do it, the better. Your phone can be tracked too, you know." Of course, she was irritatingly right.

Everything's great. You guys having fun? I texted Janet.

Yes! A change in scenery and some stress-free time did us real good. But we're still worried. How are you doing?

Never better. You take your time and stay as long as you want. Everything's good. No worries.

Don't forget to send me your school report tomorrow.

Oh, no. School reports are released on Friday, the last day before break. I totally forgot.

Sure, I texted, feeling much worse.

Avery dropped by the house this evening, but no one was there. She sent me a text, but I can't reach her. I totally forgot about the check-in. Can you call and meet up with her?

Avery was my social worker, and her monthly visit was scheduled for tomorrow. Because I was an adopted orphan, it was required for me to have an appointment with her every month. Ugh.

And if she didn't see me or ever suspected that I was about to leave the Jacobs... My parents could be in real trouble, not only with Avery but with the courts, too. As I thought more about it, it could also draw Opal's attention, too.

For some reason, Avery didn't like Janet, and no way was I letting the social worker badmouth my mother. If anyone was at fault, it was me. I'd call Avery and give hints that I was restless and eager for adventure. Maybe tell her that I was going to that summer camp she kept mentioning. So, when I went missing according to plan, she wouldn't blame Janet.

Oh, no, no. Dammit. I scrolled through my contacts list. I didn't have Avery's number saved. It would be on the fridge at home. I couldn't ask Janet. She'd know I wasn't home. I sent her a quick goodnight and promised to keep her updated (I made sure I remained vague about my school report).

Shame and regret came over me. I hadn't been very good to my parents, but so far, I'd never lied to them like this before.

"Be quiet," Ash hissed.

She was probably right. I couldn't tell if she was referring to my thoughts or my phone that made a little noise every time I typed. I quickly tucked it away. The three of us were already quiet, moving around the branches and twigs.

Lost in my thoughts, I didn't notice that Ash stopped until I bumped into her backpack. Flame steadied me, then gasped as she withdrew her hand. In the darkness, I saw Ash throw her a warning look.

"What is it?" I whispered.

"Can you hear that?" Ash replied.

We stood in a clearing. I listened hard, but other than the slight rustling and scrambling in the bushes—usual noises in the forest—I discerned nothing. The branches above us formed a canopy, and only a few rays of moonlight filtered through. I couldn't see a damn thing, either.

For a moment, we were still. Then Ash cast a glare at my hands, and I stiffened under the intensity. I shoved my hands in my pockets, suddenly aware of the glow they emitted. But it was too late. I froze.

The red light lit up dozens of glowing eyes. Beastly eyes surrounded us.

I swallowed and looked down at my hands again, but the tendrils had mostly disappeared. No shield, no energy wave. Ash and Flame stood back-to-back instinctively, ready to fight.

"If any of them attack," Ash whispered, "I'll take the ones at three o'clock. I can pick up at least a dozen rocks to throw. Flame, you take the ones at seven o'clock with your blast. Michael... um, just do what you can to stay alive. Where's your shield? Argh, never mind. Just, whatever you do... Don't. Get. Bitten."

Yeah, Michael. Why can't you manifest your shield at will?

I nodded and then realized they couldn't see me. "What's going on?"

"Wolves," Ash said quietly. "We're surrounded by wolves and werewolves."

CHAPTER 17

Werewolves? A low growl somewhere on my right echoed in the clearing, and I jumped. So, when Ash insisted on the don't-get-bitten part, she meant it. What would happen if I did? I didn't want to find out.

"Some of them aren't normal wolves," Ash whispered. "You don't want to become a werewolf." Was she reading my mind again? I was too flustered—and terrified—right now to tell her off.

Werewolves. Like shapeshifters? My days were getting weirder and weirder. When was I going to catch a damn break?

"Next, you're going to tell me vampires exist, too," I retorted.

"Vampires aren't real, moron. Focus. They're getting ready to attack."

As my eyes adjusted to the darkness, I noticed the glinting eyes narrowing. Low growls cut into the silence from different angles. That snapped my thoughts into a million pieces. Shoot. I couldn't even see the shield.

"Ash?" Flame said in a small voice. Tiny blue plasma flickered from her fingers. In the glow, I saw her hands quiver slightly. "There are too many of them."

Just when I thought that nothing scared her.

I scooted closer. Heat emanated from her, and her eyes were wide. Her panic mode was full-on. Could I produce a shield to protect us? I could only hope the wolves would lose interest in us, but the odds of that seemed low right now.

To my surprise, when the light from Flame's hands lit up mine, I saw no waves radiating from them. Not even a red tendril. Was my mana completely depleted, or were the wolves not a threat? Maybe there was a nullifier nearby. No, Flame's blue sparks were in full blast. What was happening?

Ash whispered to Flame, "Keep your sparks under control, sis. We don't want to make the first move. Michael, stay still. Your fidgeting is setting them on edge, I think. Just be ready."

Ready for what? With a dozen wolf-like eyes surrounding us, I felt vulnerable without my shield. I could hardly defend myself with my fists against a single person, let alone wolves. Make that at least a dozen.

"I don't think they mean us any harm," I said uncertainly. "My shield—"

"Is that an opinion or a fact?" Ash countered, an edge in her voice. "Chances are, they're ready to kill us." Her eyes shifted to me for a moment, and she growled in annoyance. "And stay still!"

I was bouncing from foot to foot, twigs crunching under my foot. My fidgeting increased with my nervousness. The glowing eyes were unnerving. It seemed to me the wolves had no intention of attacking us. Or were they waiting for something?

Despite her words, Ash looked like she was about to start the attack the longer we stood around.

A wolf with amber eyes advanced, separating itself from the line of yellow eyes. The shape elongated, startling all three of us. Flame gasped, and the blue flickers of plasma disappeared. I cringed, watching the shapeshifting wolf, catching a peek of a bare shoulder.

To our shock, a girl in her teens stood before us, wearing dirty overalls (to my relief, as I was the only boy present).

"A wolf-shifter," Flame trembled. Blue sparks sputtered from her hands and sizzled on the ground. A few jumped in the air, one of them brushing past the wolf-girl's hair. The latter hissed as parts of her brown hair blackened.

"Stand down, Flame," Ash said in a firm tone. She raised her hand and stepped in front of her sister. The sparks subsided.

"Maybe we should've taken the longer road," Flame mumbled in a sullen voice. "I didn't read anything human nearby, so I figured..."

"Human read..." the wolf-girl said, glancing at the blue sparks. "You has Meta abilities! I was wolf for long time."

"You can speak!" Ash said in awe.

Apparently, a girl who could shapeshift into a wolf was normal. But one who could also speak was unusual?

"I was human-child before I turn wolf." She touched her face with one hand, while the other raised waist-high. "I was this tall. Lots of hair now. Ma and Pa make me come here and wait. This is my place. I stay in woods. Why you come here?"

"We're heading to a base," Ash replied. "A place where humans with abilities can get help. Shapeshifters are welcome, too. Those who cannot control their gifts."

"Gifts?" A bitter laugh came from the wolf-shifter. "Ma and Pa scared of gift. Everyone scared of me. They make me go away."

She took a step forward, and her features came into the light. She had pointed wolf ears, frizzy brown hair on her shoulders, and tanned skin. Something swished behind her, which I assumed to be a tail.

I steeled myself not to recoil when I saw her hand

on her face. Curved, long fingernails like claws rubbed at her chin. She smiled, and I swallowed at her fangs and pointed teeth.

"That base help...people like me? I want to see it."

"Are you the alpha of your pack?" Ash asked. "The base is across the woods. Tell your pack we mean no harm. We're not hunters."

"Alpha...like leader? Yes, yes."

Suddenly, she whipped her head toward me, her amber eyes like a dagger. Her small smile disappeared. "My...pack smell things. Wolf smell something wrong, maybe danger. Something is coming. You hear that?"

I listened, but nothing other than the rustling of leaves reached my ears.

"I can sense the little animals' fear," Ash murmured.

"I can sense my wolves' fear. They want to protect... But what?" The wolf-girl was still staring at me and narrowed her eyes. She sniffed, her body looming toward me. I forced myself to stay still. "Who is the boy? What he want with my wolves?"

Three pairs of curious female eyes converged on me. Not in a flattering way.

"You said the wolves meant us no harm," Ash said. "How did you know?"

"Uh..." It was hard to think with so many prying eyes. I lifted my hands. The wolves around us shifted at my movement. "No shield. It usually forms when there's danger." The wolves seemed to be nodding their heads.

"You!" the girl said, frowning. "My wolves answer you. That's not possible—" She stopped abruptly. "I fight you."

"What?" I said. An involuntary nervous chuckle spills from my mouth. "Me?"

Ash and Flame were looking at me, confused.

"Yes, you. New...alpha. I fight alpha before, and now I'm alpha. So I fight you. Alpha before was old and slow. You're young. Like me. It's good fight."

A vicious smile stretched her lips, perhaps at the memory of the fight. I had absolutely no intention of fighting her. With her claws and fangs, I didn't have a single chance. And...what did she mean by 'new alpha'? I wasn't even a wolf, darn it.

"I'm not an alpha. Or...or a wolf," I said. I didn't care that I was pleading. When the wolf-girl didn't say anything, I tried again. "Here, uh...I resign as your wolves' leader. Happy? We just want to get across the forest and reach the base."

"I don't think you can just leave," Ash started slowly. "If she's right, then you're the pack's leader now."

"Leave?" the wolf-girl shrieked. "No, no, no. He not leave. Wolves—my wolves—follow him everywhere. No, rule is rule. He must fight."

She brought her fists up. I looked at my hands. Not a

single wave. Apparently, my shield went on vacation. But that girl was an extreme threat to my safety!

Suddenly, the wolf-girl straightened up. She brought her face toward the sky and sniffed. The wolves surrounding us scattered and whimpered.

"I thought you was danger, but there's something more," the girl said, bringing one hand to her ear. "You hear that? Nothing. Wood not like that. No bird, no rabbit, no buzz. I live here long time. Never see wood like that. Never!"

Ash swallowed. She turned to us, eyes widened in fear. "She's right. Something's wrong. We have to move away from here fast. I can—"

A bright light cut her off, illuminating the woods. My red shield burst from my hands. About time. But not soon enough. Ugh.

"Run!" Ash screamed. "Flame, grab Michael!"

She bolted toward the line of trees. Flame was right on her heels, stretching her hand toward me. I automatically reached out. Our fingertips touched. But she flinched, and before I could get a hold of her, a mop of hair flanked by two pointed ears barreled onto my back. I fell forward, planting my face into the wet, soggy ground. Bright pinpoints of blue light appeared in my vision.

I blinked. The bright light didn't go away. It became brighter, almost blinding.

I lifted my head up, my gaze searching for Flame, holding out my hand in front of me. But she was too far away. Before her was a swirling green wave. Like a portal. Ash's body vanished into it. Flame's desperate eyes met mine before she was pulled inside as well.

A portal? Teleportation? I huffed in frustration. Ash didn't mention that ability. How much was she hiding from me? How could I trust her if she just abandoned me in the dark?

Unless... Unless this was the Mage's doing. Karma. I recalled Ash was holding onto the pendant when she disappeared into the ether, pulling Flame along.

I groaned. Red waves swirled around me in full force.

Still lying on the ground, with a wolf-girl tackling me and a blinding light rocketing toward us, I flung my forearms forward as hard as I could. The shield responded to me as if it could read my mind and formed a dome around us.

I closed my eyes as the full force of the blast crashed on top of the shield. My arms trembled, the heat around us scorching my bare skin. The wolf-girl whimpered—she must be getting the full brunt of the heat on her—but I didn't let go of the shield. If I did, we would die.

I waited and waited, arms trembling and body aching, until the light behind my eyelids receded. A blue hue to the light unnerved me, but there was no time to contemplate that.

I sensed a faint presence nearby as I stilled, eyes shut and waiting, but I had no choice except to ignore it and focus on keeping the shield up.

At least five minutes passed until I exhaled deeply, releasing the shield. The presence was gone. How strange.

The shield slowly retracted, the pull on my arms slowly fading. An acrid smell burnt my nostrils, and my eyes burned, the tears blurring my vision. The wolf-girl was already up and running into the surrounding darkness, shrieking. I turned around with effort to see that she began to glow bright orange, shapeshifting into a wolf as she sprinted away.

I staggered to my feet and grabbed my bag. Fortunately, it had landed under the dome.

A howl echoed in the woods. It went on and on, and for some inexplicable reason, my chest ached, the despair and sadness in that single wail so heart-wrenching.

Thoughts scrambled in my mind, and I didn't know what to do. I was alone in the woods. I didn't know if I should trust Ash or where to find the base. I didn't know what the blinding light was.

My feet were unsteady, my shield gone. I was unsure whether I had enough mana to manifest another one. My last attempt took quite a toll on my body.

I took one step, then another, but something stopped

me. My sixth sense was back again, warning me. I recognized the hitch in my throat, the hair rising at the back of my neck, and the familiar ache in my chest. I took out my phone and tried to turn the flashlight on. My fingers shook so much that the phone couldn't catch my tactile movements.

That was when I saw wisps of smoke swirling up from the ground. Blackened stumps scattered around me. Worse, five steps from where I stood was a crater. My flashlight lit it up. It must be at least ten feet deep.

What was the blinding blue light? Clearly, it'd caused the explosion that formed the crater. And the crater... It was right where the three of us had stood only moments earlier. Before Ash told us to run.

I backed away, staggering. I could've fallen into that giant crater, straight to my death. I found it hard to focus on my next step.

Another howl echoed, louder this time. I got to my feet again. An immediate threat called for immediate action, and that was the wolf-girl. She still intended to take me down. I needed to move, get out of these damn woods.

My thoughts raced through my options. I could go back to my house, but Rimes would have his minions there. Westview was definitely a no-no. Go to the base and wait it out? I had no idea where to find the base.

No, I needed to find Ash and Flame first. Make sure

they were safe. Ash had called out for Flame to take my hand. She might be annoying, but she still meant to protect me. They must be worried.

Where could they be? I could only think of their house, protected by that charm. Maybe the girls tele-ported there. Where was it again? Stupid me. I didn't pay any heed to the exact location. All I could remember was that it was close to the mall and the parking lot. Reming-ton? Lexington? No, wait, it was on Islington Avenue.

I retraced my steps, focusing on a distant light at the top of an apartment complex. My sixth sense sent a warning through me. As I glanced around the scenery of the forest, I had a strange feeling that I was being followed. But no one was around, and the whistling of the wind was all I heard.

I found a pair of glowing eyes staring at me a dozen steps away. Something hung from the wolf's mouth. In-stinctively, I knew it was a mother wolf carrying its cub. I didn't know whether the cub was alive or not, but it remained unmoving.

What I knew for sure was that the wolf meant no harm. A mysterious sadness washed over me. Tears stung my eyes, but I blinked them away, a lump forming in my throat. The wolf lowered its muzzle. By the time I realized it was bowing, it had already darted past me and disappeared into the darkness. It occurred to me that the sadness I felt was from the mother wolf. Was I really connected to these wolves?

I shook my head. How could they change alphas so suddenly? How could I be a pack leader? I'd done nothing to deserve the title. Worse, I'd failed to protect these wolves when the explosion happened. How many of them died?

No, the wolves weren't my responsibility. I could barely be responsible for my own safety. I resolved to find Ash and Flame. That was my priority. Nothing else.

My phone buzzed. Was it how I—we—were tracked? Because I didn't ditch my phone when I was asked to? With trembling hands, I shut off my phone.

The howls followed me as I headed toward the dark alleys of Golden Birch's industrial park.

CHAPTER 18

My ears still didn't pick up any unusual sounds, but my sixth sense warned me I was being followed. The footsteps were light, and when I whipped around more than a few times, I saw nothing but shadows. I almost thought I was paranoid. Almost. There was no warning shield around my hands, but then again, I didn't have to check my mana to know I was too darn exhausted to fight anything right now.

My steps took me back to Broadway Park—Islington must be close by, I guessed. I needed to be somewhere familiar. Too much had happened too fast. I was physically and mentally exhausted, and all I wanted was to rest on that bench.

But first, I needed to lose my stalker.

It was easier to track the light footsteps on the grass. My body wasn't on alert, so I also could safely assume that my stalker meant me no harm, or else they would've incapacitated me by now. Not an Opal agent, then. That intrigued me most. Who could it be? And why all the sneaking around?

I settled on a bench and pretended to watch the dark horizon and leaves fluttering against the sky. As the footsteps moved closer, I ducked behind the bench and backtracked behind the tree.

Sure enough, my stalker leaned against a tree, a mere shadow. Then, the smell hit me. It was a dead giveaway.

"Why are you following me?" My voice cut into the silence, startling the shadow. It whirled around, and the wolf-girl was staring at me. In the clear moonlight, I could see the muddy streaks on her cheeks where tears had formed a clear path. Her overalls were even filthier under the moonlight. She swiped at the tangled mass of dark hair over her face before replying.

"You alpha," she answered. Which wasn't really an answer. "I follow you."

"I'm not." I clenched my fists, barely stopping myself from crying out. "Do I look like a leader to you? Look at me. I have no home, nothing except whatever's in this dumb backpack. No family. No friends. I have no clue where to go and certainly no clue how to look after a pack of wolves. If I were an alpha, I should've protected the pack, right? But I didn't. Get away from me! I got enough on my hands."

Somehow, my survival skills were failing me. Part of

me knew she could rip me with her claws any time to reclaim her status as alpha. Still, I was too darn tired and overwhelmed to worry about an attack. And she didn't look as vicious as she had before. She was too calm, and I sensed a certain dejection from her. A sense of loss. She was trying hard to keep it together. I could relate to that. I had lost a lot in one day—I almost felt bad for snapping at her.

"I has no family, no friends too," she finally said. "The wolves came to protect you. Protect alpha. And died. Now I protect you, too."

Her tone was matter-of-fact, as if it were normal. As if everything that happened was normal. But I sensed that she was trying to comfort me as well as she could. "All I has was wolves. Now, they no listen to me. They listen to you. Obey you. I has no one."

My heart ached at the loneliness in her words. First, her parents gave her up for being different, and now the wolves for no reason. She was in a worse situation than me. The thought brought Janet and Mark to mind. I was lucky to be with selfless parents who cared about me—not all parents were that great.

Wolf-girl had known none of that. My self-pity faded away.

I never understood the whole glass half empty, glass half full conundrum Mark used to talk about. Now

I did. I had to change my outlook and consider the glass-half-full scenario. I was unhurt. I had clothes. I had a backpack full of resources, and a few twenty-dollar bills. On top of that, I could protect myself with my shield. I was luckier than most, for now.

I straightened up. "Since you're not fighting me, maybe we can come up with a truce. Let's start with names. I'm Michael."

"Truce? I am Tempest Silver." Then she frowned. "What Michael mean?"

I bit my lip. "Not sure. A name is a name. It doesn't define who you are."

Tempest's eyebrows dug deeper. "Names important. My name before—" She faltered, then recovered. "Why you alpha? I not understand."

"I don't understand either, Tempest. I didn't ask for this ability. I didn't ask to be an alpha." I moved to the bench and noticed Tempest's ears were almost human-like. Even better was the absence of a tail.

"Who are you, Michael?"

"Just an ordinary boy who goes to school," I replied, counting on my fingers, "who loves his science homework and gets bullied. Regular teen stuff."

"School..." she said. "I know school. Why you leader?"

Maybe she hadn't heard me just now. Maybe she needed a good reason for losing her family. I just didn't know any.

"Why don't you stick with me?" I blurted out. Shoot. My mouth seemed to have different ideas from my brain. Again.

Her gaze swept to my backpack, hesitating. "Stick?"

"I mean, stay with me until we find somewhere to stay. We're both lost and have no one. We can keep each other company."

Her fists clenched. "Like a mate?"

I was so glad it was dark at night, and she couldn't see my flushed face. "No! Geez, I'm fourteen." She looked confused again. "I just asked you to be friends until we find my other two friends. You want to go to the base, too, right?"

The mention of the base lit up her eyes. I blew out a sigh of relief. "Friends? I like friends. I want friend with alpha. What is base?"

I was somewhat glad she'd followed me for friendship and seemed to have abandoned the idea of attacking me to regain her alpha status.

"Base is where friends help each other. You hungry?" I asked. After the dome shield I produced in the forest, I was famished. "I have sandwiches."

I had an inkling that she already knew my backpack held food. Her gaze strayed to it again, eyes wide. She licked her lips.

I took out two of the packed sandwiches. I wondered whether the vegetarian slices would be to her taste. What did wolves hunt and eat anyway? The image of raw, bloody meat came forth in my mind, but I pushed the thought away. I was too tired to feel disgusted.

Unsurprisingly, she wolfed (pun intended) the sandwich down in two bites, not bothering to chew, and stared at the backpack. "More?"

"Got to ration it, Tempest," I answered. When she frowned at my words, I shook my head, watching her shoulders slump. "We'll head to my friends' house. Maybe they teleported there." Tempest looked more interested in my backpack than in finding shelter. "Maybe there'll be food in the house. I'd love some ice cream." I added the last part in, recalling the awful heat.

"Cream?" Tempest's eyes widened slowly. "I like cream. I don't like house."

"We need shelter for the night."

Tempest patted the bench and sat with crossed legs.

"Nope, I'm not sleeping on a bench," I said firmly. She looked confused and pointed at the tree.

"Nope," I repeated. "I've done all that stuff before. Slept in parks and under trees, in dirty alleyways. We can't do that now; it's not hygienic. Plus, it's cold out. C'mon. Let's find Ash and Flame—the two girls who were with me. I need to know if they're safe. Also, you really need a bath," Tempest wrinkled her nose at the last word. She seemed to understand what it meant.

Maybe we'd even find Karma. She seemed to have all the answers, and I had too many questions. From what Ash said, she would protect us.

"Protect… No more protect wolf. No more pack." She huffed. Tempest's tone was even, but regret washed over me. I flinched. I didn't like sensing her emotions like this. It was too overwhelming, too confusing. Wait, was it my confusion, or—argh, never mind.

I picked up my backpack and headed toward the street where I'd fought Mole-Man. Damn, that fight felt like it happened ages ago. Strange. Suddenly, I froze and turned to her as the realization dawned on me. "I didn't say anything."

"Say what?" She shrugged, distracted by a flock of ravens in the sky.

"I thought of 'protect'. I didn't say it."

"You thought of protect. You didn't say it. Good?"

She was parroting me and had no clue what I meant. I closed my eyes briefly, and a thought came to my head. Was it possible…?

We're heading over there, I thought, glancing to the right. *That's where my friends' house is. Islington.*

Indeed, her steps veered right. When I didn't follow, Tempest glanced at me. I didn't say a word, yet I could

AJ DASHER & KRIS RUHLER

tell she could hear me.

"You're…" I shook my head and swallowed. "You're reading my thoughts!" Somehow, the words came out as accusatory.

"No," Tempest answered in a huff. "No read. I no like read."

Yes, you're listening to me! I thought, anger surging inside me.

She smiled sweetly. "I listen. We go to house, find friends, and protect."

I sighed, my anger dropping as fast as it surged. There was no arguing with her. This wolf-girl saw no problem in reading my thoughts. Well, I had a big problem with that. I liked my privacy.

And I thought I had problems with Ash reading my mind.

All the way to Islington, I tried to block my thoughts, but it was no use.

CHAPTER 19

In the darkness of the night, with the well-kept front lawns and lit porches, every house looked the same. Which one was it? With me flustered and Tempest hopping around and staring at the buildings in fascination, we walked up and down Islington.

And then I saw it. It was a replica of every house on the street, which was good if you wanted a safe house to blend into a neighborhood. Nothing seemed unusual about it at first. Then, I discerned the eerie green and yellow glow emitting from the glassy windows.

Moonlight cast a bright shadow on the main door, painted blue. I walked down the driveway, flanked by a well-maintained green lawn and garden beds. The shrubs were clipped, and the front porch was clean and crisp. Since I'd been exhausted, I hadn't noticed much before, but now I was noticing just how orderly everything was.

Still, I hesitated to knock on the door. If Flame was there, wouldn't she have recognized me by now?

Wouldn't she have sensed my bioelectric field? But no sound came from the house.

Calling for Karma wasn't a good idea either. It would be like calling for all the bad things I've done and all the horrible thoughts I've had.

A round black dot was stuck on the door at eye level. I recognized it as a camera, the same security system as my home. Well, ex-home.

I pressed the doorbell. "You think Ash and Flame are inside?" I whispered.

"House empty," Tempest said, her bare feet kicking at some carved rocks on the porch. "They gone. Poooof!" She dramatically waved her hands in a circle.

"Teleported, yes. I was hoping that they'd be here." I paused and pressed the doorbell again. Nothing. I turned back to her. "You're sure it's empty?"

Tempest nodded, and I trusted her judgment. "Since we're already here," I said. "We might as well stay for the night. Let's check the backyard for an open door. Or open windows. They...probably won't mind us breaking in, right? Not like we're stealing anything." Once again, I was reminded of stealing from people's houses. And again, my thoughts trailed to Ben. I mentally pushed them away.

Tempest lifted one of the creepy gnome statues out front and handed me a key in silence.

I shrugged. "A key would do the job, too, I guess."

I didn't dare turn on the lights. Tempest's footsteps were confident as she went through the house. She probably had better eyesight in the dark. She stopped in the living room and stared at the pictures showing a tall woman with sleek, black hair standing between the two sisters. With emerald eyes, pale skin, and narrowed eyes, she had no resemblance to the twins.

"Tommy?" I whispered, glancing into the room where I'd last seen him. Of course, he wasn't there. It was just Tempest and me. But the house at this time of the night looked ominous like I was in an old horror movie setting. Suddenly, I was grateful I wasn't alone.

I didn't pay attention to the photos on the mantelpiece before—I guess I was so zoned out, and there was already too much to take in—but something was off.

With the moonlight seeping through a nearby window and shining down on the photos, I could see what it was. The lighting. While the right side of the sisters was in shadow, the woman's left side was darkened. The pictures were edited, of course. They didn't do a great job. Wasn't Karma supposed to be a powerful Mage?

More photo frames lined up neatly on the mantelpiece above the fireplace in the family room. Even though I knew they were fake, the sight made me ache for home. Ash and Flame were close, and I could only assume that the woman hugging them tight was their supposed guardian.

Two pictures stood out: two single frames next to each other on one side of the wall. I recognized Ash, who could be four or five, holding a frying pan like a sword as she sat there, her small legs stretching in front of her. She looked fierce and angry while sucking on the handle. Then there was Flame next to her, bawling with her mouth open, a small bruise on her shoulder. Ash must've been aiming to hit Flame on the head but missed and got her shoulder instead. I wondered what Flame had done to make Ash that mad. I was glad she hadn't hit me on the head with a frying pan. Huh, weird. I didn't see Tommy in any of the pictures.

Even though it was dark, I could now see that the house was in dire need of repair. The chain holding the chandelier hung loose. Part of the chandelier itself was shattered. The glass table was cracked, and Tempest ran a finger over the scorched parts. Flame's handiwork again.

"Your friends," Tempest said as we examined more photos on the walls.

I nodded. "We'll stay here for the night."

It was a house, not a home, despite the snippets of memories hanging around. The stairs creaked slightly as we climbed up to the first floor. I found two bathrooms and three bedrooms. Guiltily, I searched through drawers for clues about the base and the sisters' location. Most were empty.

The second bedroom was Flame's. The wallpaper on all four walls bared scorch marks and the acrid smell was a telltale sign. I now understood why Ash was so protective of her sister. She wasn't shielding her sister from the outside world.

She was shielding the outside world from her.

The third bedroom, Karma's, wasn't occupied at all. No clothes, no possessions. Only sheets and towels. I guessed Karma hadn't been around a lot.

"I know Ash and Flame from school," I said as Tempest slipped past me into the bedroom. She looked awed at the décor, sinking her hands into the mattress and leaving smudges of dirt behind. I cringed. She needed a good wash. She went on to gingerly touch as much of the furniture as she possibly could. "They were supposed to guide me to the base." I lifted my arms. "I can't control this shield, and Ash said the base will keep me safe. You've heard of Black Opal?"

Tempest shook her head. "Ash?" She lifted her singed hair. I laughed despite myself. "No, it was Flame who did that. The other girl is Ash."

"Flame. Blue sparks. You like Flame."

"Um, no," I said slowly, hoping my voice was convincing. "That's not true."

I really wished there was an off switch so she couldn't read my mind.

Suddenly, she sniffed, and I was on alert. I checked my hands for signs of danger. By the time I looked up, Tempest was heading down the stairs and turning right into the kitchen. Darn, the girl moved fast.

I flew down the stairs. She was staring at an open pizza box in awe. Ah, the pizza the girls bought for dinner. I stopped her as she lifted one hand to grab a slice. "You can't just eat other people's food!"

"No? But I'm hungry. Friends are okay. Friends share food."

Her pack of wolves shared their food alright. It seemed the sandwich we shared earlier wasn't enough for her. To be fair, it wasn't enough for me either. My stomach complained as a testament to this.

Then I decided Ash, Flame, and their guardian wouldn't mind Tempest using their bathroom either. If she was going to stay here, she might as well be presentable and hygienic.

"Okay, let's make a deal."

I was relieved that she knew the intricate details about bathing. Her sharp, dirty nails had to be clipped. I cringed as I did them for her and then handed her clean jeans and tee- shirt from one of the girls' rooms. I had no idea if they'd fit her.

I promised her half the pizza if she got herself clean. And that was a winning deal. Hopefully, there was more food around. I walked into the kitchen and checked the cupboards. All of them were bare, as expected. Ash and Flame must not have made it to the grocery store. Perhaps they'd only bought the pizza.

Sure, the two sisters were on the skinny side, but this was downright ridiculous. Anyone looking at these cupboards would think the place was deserted. The only foods there were packets of sugar and ketchup from fast-food outlets. Not sure if those even qualified as foods.

My last resort was digging into my bag's supplies. Then, I remembered the Rocky Road ice cream. I decided to check the fridge first. Nothing, as I expected. But a dark shadow caught my eye. There was something else in that fridge. I almost staggered back as I pried the metal back open.

Two shelves in the fridge were stacked with *weapons*. Daggers, bows, knives, even a couple of guns, and—wait, were those...axes?

Why would someone hide weapons inside their fridge? Who needed a gun when they could shoot blue plasma out of their fingers? I mean, yes, there were nullifiers, but why guns? I mean, sure, Opal agents might be looking for them, but their guardian shouldn't be leaving *guns* in the possession of two teenagers. Even the knives constituted a hazard.

Now, don't get me wrong. I'd seen guns before. I'd broken into people's homes before, but I never expected to end up breaking into a home with a *key* and finding *weapons* rather than food inside the fridge. This was absurd.

Underneath the kitchen countertop and the coffee table in the living room were daggers taped to the bottom of the surface. Suddenly, the house didn't feel safe anymore. I could only conclude that Ash, Flame, and their guardian had these safety precautions because they expected to be attacked anytime, despite the charm around the house.

As I opened the freezer, I instinctively braced myself, hoping there would be normal frozen foods (no severed fingers, limbs, or heads, like in the movies). The four frozen muffins and piles of Rocky Road ice cream were normal enough.

But the eight metal spheres inside appeared to be bombs. I had no clue what the cylindrical tubes could be. I was no expert, so I quickly took out two frozen muffins and a tub of ice cream. Those were for dessert.

What a weird house. A weird house for weird people, I guess. The muffins were larger than my fist, so I smushed two onto a plate and microwaved them.

A howl cut into the silence. Heart pounding, I rushed up the stairs and knocked on the bathroom door. My mind whirled with possibilities. What could possibly make her howl like that? Were we under attack?

"Tempest? Tempest! Are you okay?"

A string of curses followed, most of them directed at the waters and something about the changing water temperature. I blew out a sigh of relief. Wolves didn't seem to like water that much.

I walked back to the kitchen, wincing at the sound of crashes and thudding from the bathroom. While nibbling casually on one of the enormous chocolate chip muffins, I thought about the mess I'd have to clean up.

As soon as Tempest got into Flame's room, I flew up the stairs to the bathroom with a pile of towels and drying cloths. It felt like an old routine at my old home. It was one thing my foster parents loved about me: I cleaned up well after myself, and I liked things in their proper place.

That was why the weapons in the fridge bothered me so much. They shouldn't be in the fridge. But I had no clue where people usually kept their guns and knives; and technically, this wasn't my house.

The bathroom was clean and gleaming by the time I got downstairs. Tempest was still getting ready. It didn't bother me. In movies, people took a long time to get dressed. They never explained why. I'd probably never understand why, either.

When Tempest came downstairs, I hardly recognized her. Once she was cleaned up, she looked a lot better. Her brown hair was wet and tousled, and her skin was smooth and unblemished. I heard mud made a good exfoliator. Her shirt was back to front with the label sticking out; her dark blue jeans fit her well and...were unzipped. Of course, I immediately shifted my eyes back to her face. Her cheeks were flushed, and I wondered whether she was ill. She was holding a hand to her cheek.

"Did you hurt yourself?" I asked awkwardly.

"That soap!" The words came out as an angry growl. "It slips and slips. How you hold it? I catch it, then it drops." Her eyes narrowed further. "No more bath!"

"All right. I'll...look for soap that doesn't slip."

"How you get this to tie?" she muttered, pointing to the zipper.

I kept my eyes stuck to her face. "Uh, find some leggings or something without buttons or a zipper."

Suddenly, Tempest looked to the side and beamed. "Cake for me?"

"It's a muffin, actually. Found it—" Tempest had already munched down half of the muffin in two bites. I cleared my throat. "—in the freezer. Well, you can have the pizza as promised. Leave the rest for breakfast. That's all the food I can find in this place, other than the three tubs of ice cream. Uh, just be careful. There's some weird stuff in there. Like weapons? Probably best if we don't touch them."

"Ice...cream?"

I opened the freezer door. "Yes, three tubs. Rocky Road flavor. Wanna try it?"

I finished my muffin, and when I looked up, Tempest was staring at the open freezer, eyes teary. "Tempest? You okay? I have candies in my bag—"

She ignored me and picked up a tub that sat right next to a metallic sphere...or bomb. Whatever it was. But she was totally unfazed. At least she had the sense to look for a spoon before she started eating it in large chunks.

As expected, she got a brain freeze. Through the pain and tears, she laughed. It was so loud that it made me smile.

"Eat slowly," I told her.

"Ma give me Rocky Road on Sundays," she said between mouthfuls, smiling at the thought. "Is it Sunday?"

"No, it's Thursday. Or...maybe Friday?" I sighed. "If my friends don't turn up by tomorrow morning, I think we should leave this place. There's not much food and no point staying here." I already mentioned the weapons in the house, but I doubted she was paying any attention to my words other than the mention of ice cream. "Tomorrow, we'll head back to my house early. I need to get a phone number."

"You need phone?"

"Yep. Then we'll head into the woods again. I mean, how far can the base be?"

"So, you have house. Why you stay here in friends' house?"

"It's complicated." She looked confused, so I tried to explain. "Let's just say some bad guys are after me. So tomorrow, we'll go see if it's safe."

Tempest yawned and dropped her spoon, already bored with the subject. I put the ice cream back in the freezer.

"We go sleep now," Tempest said. "Too dark out there."

I looked around and pointed to the couch. "I'll get us some blankets." A warm feeling came over me. "No shifting, okay? You'll get fur everywhere."

It was near the end of the winter months, and it was cool. Tempest was probably used to sleeping outside in the cold. That wasn't something I was looking forward to. Another reason I needed to find that base and get to safety.

I found a couple of blankets. Intact ones, that is, with no blackened marks and holes. When I reached the bottom of the stairs, a soft snore reached my ears. I found

Tempest sleeping on the rug, her knees curled up to her chest. I draped one of the blankets over her, then curled onto the sofa opposite her.

It was late, and exhaustion flooded me. Yet, I couldn't find sleep. Images of Ben came rushing at me even as I tried to block them out.

The past few hours had been draining. I could never go back to my past life now. At least Flame—and Ash, in some way—had been there for me after what happened at Westview.

Caring for Flame made me feel good, even though she could take good care of herself. Caring for Tempest made me feel good, too. If I could reject that weird alpha status, I'd do it without a second thought. Maybe there was a reason the wolves saw me as their alpha. Maybe there was a reason that shield became a part of me.

Yet, another part of me resented that shield. Everything was different now. As a kid, I'd learned to survive on my own, and now I had to do it again.

As sleep claimed me, I vowed that, with these new abilities, I'd do some good. Like my parents had taught me.

Hopefully, I'd see the Jacobs, Ash, and Flame again.

CHAPTER 20

The Overworld

T he energy from a single orb barely kept the Aequus alive. Cocooned in its shell, it rested for days that were mere minutes on Earth. The Aequus quickly realized it would need more orbs, more energy, more food. So, while resting, it launched its plan into motion.

Aboveground was the Mages' portal. Though their battle was no longer raging, the Aequus didn't trust these beings, even the Mages who awakened it. In fact, it didn't know who to trust. After all, it had battled a few Mages before they sent it to this wretched place.

Did the portal lead to the human-Child's world? There was only one way to find out: burst through the tons of rocks, get to the portal, and use the Mages to open it.

But to do that, the Aequus needed energy and allies. So, with its telepathic radar, it searched for all the creatures and found Krauk, the leader of the Kura'Ki.

Before it had been defeated, the Aequus had sworn

gifts to the Kura'Ki. Their army used to be in the billions, swarming their planet. As the Aequus's projected gaze swept over the Kura'Ki planet, it noted their numbers were greatly depleted from a lack of resources.

The Aequus decided that the Children's planet, though, was a much better one: not so desolate and a place where the Kura'Ki could stay and enjoy the fresh water, clean air, and food that was lacking in their current one.

Through its telepathy, the Aequus showed the Kura'Ki how the Children's planet could be their new habitat. A little tweak to tick the temperature up, and it was the ideal planet for the swarm of Kura'Ki. The Earthlings were already doing well enough with increasing the temperature on their own. They just needed a little push.

Krauk was easily convinced. The Kura'Ki leader stood, entranced with blank eyes like a wasp's and devoid of expression, watching the Children's planet. Saliva flooded its mouth at the food spread out for it to take. It flapped its well-built muscular wings carved on its back, shaped like that of a giant fly.

Then, it turned to its fellow comrades and cackled orders. It would lead its people to the green planet with forests to live in, animals to consume, and lots of water. It would conquer the Children's planet for its people.

The Aequus projected an image to the Mages above

of the Kura'Ki's destination. It waited, then grinned when a portal opened for the Kura'Ki allies.

How gullible were these Mages.

The Aequus watched through Krauk's eyes as it flew through the portal and pounced on the Mages. The Aequus delighted with the Kura'Ki's vociferous hunger as they devoured the weakened Mages. They had served their purpose of awakening it. But they sought to control it, and the Aequus would never be controlled.

More orbs appeared, dangling from the roots. The Aequus's forked tail lashed out and seized them. Ah, the Kura'Ki understood the Aequus's hunger and did its bidding very well. Kill the Mages and give their Great Leader many orbs. They would be compensated for their loyalty soon.

Krauk found the Mages' portal and flew in at the Aequus's direction. It turned out to be the Mages' planet, not the Child's. But what Krauk found was more precious: thousands more orbs! At its bidding, Krauk started gathering them in a pile.

The Aequus grinned in its sleep, its plans now in motion. It projected itself on the Child's planet—Earth, as it was called—seeking the human, the living reincarnation of the one who had defeated and buried it. It sought and sought until it found another human—a so-called Commander Rimes—and watched through his eyes. The Commander was seeking the Child, too, for his own purposes. Pleased, the Aequus projected the image of Commander Rimes to Krauk.

Gather your armies, the Aequus's voice projected into the minds of the two leaders. *The End is near. But my true enemy, that human child, will defend this Earth well. You will rise and make history. You will have more than plenty. But not until you take down that Child first.*

It projected an image of the Child sitting on a pile of debris near a tall building.

That Child was the Essence of all good in the Multiverse, but the weak reincarnation of his enemy didn't understand that winning mattered above everything else. Disgust filled the Aequus, the harbinger of all evil and utter destruction. Once it absorbed all the orbs and replenished its energy, nothing—not even this weakened Child—would stop it.

It waited patiently, watching the events from its telepathic radar. It waited for the Kura'Ki to gather more orbs. Then, it recalled that its defeat occurred because one of the Children had a precognitive ability. But this time, it was sure that it would win.

No one would see the Great Aequus coming.

Thanks for Reading!

Did you enjoy this book?

Want to help spread the word?

Please consider leaving a review.

As indie authors, we don't have big promotional budgets and rely almost completely on word-of-mouth and reviews to help spread the word about our work.

Reviews where the book is sold, in addition to places such as Goodreads, BookBub, blogs, and other review websites, can help readers discover what we're doing, so we appreciate anything you can do to help!

So if you want others to enjoy Rise of Legends as you have, please leave a short note, even if it's just a few words to say that you really like this book.

amazon.com/Kris-Ruhler/e/B09WPM19BP/

goodreads.com/author/show/22325810.Kris_Ruhl er

[BB] bookbub.com/authors/kris-ruhler

Reviews are invaluable for a new writer and make a huge difference!

Interested to know when the next book comes out? Pop over to krisruhler.com and sign up to my mailing list.

You'll get updates about new releases as well as exclusive promotions

I'd love to have you!

Thanks again for reading!

Acknowledgements

Thank you to everyone who contributed to the making of this book. I mean everyone, including you, who picked up this book and took a chance on a new author.

So, my dear reader, thank you. Reading my work makes me so happy.

I truly owe thanks to my friends and family, who listen to me rant about Chosen Legends and complain about the writing process (seriously, why is it so hard to write??)

And thank you to everyone who sends me cat videos or pictures of their pets. You have no idea how much it brightens my day and motivates me to work hard.

And for you, my fellow writer or author, believe in your writing. Trust that it will work out. And if it doesn't the first time, try again. Don't give up just yet!

-AJ

A big THANK YOU to all my readers. You keep me writing far into the night. And it's a good thing. it makes everything worthwhile when you follow your passion.

-Kris

ABOUT AJ

 AJ Dasher is a YA author from outer space (just kidding, she's from Ontario, Canada). Her floppy train of thought never stops running, and nor will her love for books. If she isn't writing down nonsensical ideas on paper (in messy handwriting, of course), she will likely find herself sleeping on the job, creating abstract art, or playing piano.

She loves sushi, Chinese food, and, *voila*, playing games in her free time.

"Books are like people—some will be good and some will be bad. It's all about looking for the ones you will love and remember." - AJ Dasher

ABOUT KRIS

Kris grew up reading classic novels to her mother. From these moments, she became fascinated with books and words. It was always the gritty worlds and the characters' growth that drew her in, and she often found herself engrossed in young adult science fiction, dystopian, and fantasy.

A lifelong daydreamer, she finally decided to put down her dreams onto paper. She tried to write straight science fiction and then straight fantasy, but both never clicked. So now she creates worlds just a tad bit different from ours - a blend of the futuristic with a touch of the fantastic. Like so, *Strands of* Time, her debut novel and the first book in the Aeterna Chronicles, was born.

Kris holds a degree in psychology and lives in rural Ontario, Canada, with her husband and four children.

If you have any questions or comments about any of her works, she would love to hear from you, even if it's only to drop by to say hello

krisruhler.com

Connect with me at the following:

Social Media

instagram.com/krisruhler/

facebook.com/krisruhlerauthor/

https://twitter.com/KrisRuhler

Author Pages

amazon.com/Kris-Ruhler/e/B09WPM19BP/

bookbub.com/authors/kris-ruhler

goodreads.com/author/show/22325810.Kris_Ruhler

Start the Next Book

Threads of Illusion

Chosen Legends Book 2: Threads of Illusion

Coming late 2023

Turn the page and Start Reading.....

PROLOGUE

When the Skirmisher's eyes flew open, they almost immediately fluttered closed again in exhaustion. He felt drowsy and weak as if he'd been drugged. *I probably was,* he thought, as his limbs refused to move. He was in complete darkness, apart from the faint red glow before him. But he didn't need to see anything to understand what was happening.

Thick, steel rings clasped his wrists and ankles to a concrete wall. His back ached, and his muscles strained and tensed. He couldn't even move his neck since a loose ring was around it, preventing him from turning his head. A mask covered his nose and mouth, and his breaths came out in low hisses.

The red glow emanated from small tube-like objects placed around him like candles as if he were in a sacrifice ritual. Considering his situation, he might as well have been. But he recognized the steel objects. Nullifiers. *Advanced* nullifiers.

Not again, he thought. *Please, no.*

When the lights snapped on, he shuddered, blinded by the sudden change in lighting behind his eyelids. When he finally pried his eyes open, he glimpsed several figures watching him. He felt uncomfortable—even in his weakened state, he could sense their fear.

Fear of him.

He recognized his friend Clarity and their superiors, Lyra and Raiden. In front of them was Commander Rimes, who remained silent in contemplation, most likely. The Skirmisher stiffened under Rimes' cold gaze. It hurt to swallow, but he did anyway.

And then the memories came flooding back, in long waves drowning him. Howls of wounded wolves echoed in his mind. Silver smoke and bright cobalt flames swallowed leafless trees. Charred trunks felled within seconds. The Skirmisher had no control over what he had done.

The flames stilled abruptly, left in a lingering motion. The smoke ceased to rise, and the Skirmisher waved his hand through the wisps. Nothing happened. Strange.

Before him, a pair of twins were running, their movements slowed in the vision. Both have dark hair and hazel eyes, he notices. One of them reaches out to a boy around the same age. The boy reaches out to her, too. Their fingers barely touch, but the twins vanish in a flash of rippling, green light as the boy is knocked to the ground by a wolf-girl.

The vision returned to a normal speed, and a familiar blue light flashed through the air like a sandstorm. Sapphire flames engulfed the boy and the wolf-girl.

As he gave himself a mental shake, he realized the scene before him wasn't over. The smoke was slowly clearing, and he spotted a translucent, scarlet dome in front of him. Upon closer inspection, he could make out the outlines of small, glistening triangles. Each seemed to emit a little glow, and he felt himself drawn forth, reaching out to it. His fingertips touched the dome, and it vibrated on contact. He felt a strange warmth emitting from the dome. It felt... welcome. He hadn't had that feeling in a long time.

Then, he caught sight of the still figures inside the dome. The boy from earlier and the wolf-girl. The Skirmisher stiffened but then saw their chests rising and falling in sync. There was nothing he could do to help them. This was a memory from earlier, he assumed.

He shook his head. They were Metas. His job was to kill them. And he'd failed to. A part of him was glad he'd failed. Another part of him paled at the thought of a punishment from Rimes awaiting him when he recovered.

But as he circled the dome, he caught sight of the boy's right hand. Despite the soot covering the back of it, the Skirmisher could see the faint lines of a familiar mark below the boy's pale knuckles. A circle with a triangle inside.

He clenched his teeth and cursed inwardly, staring at his own mark.

The boy was Chosen, like him. Rimes needed him alive.

He *had* to live.

Printed in Great Britain
by Amazon